JODIE FOSTER   LIAM NEESON

P9-ELP-976

Nell

TWENTIETH CENTURY FOX Presents An EGG PICTURES Production A MICHAEL APTED Film

JODIE FOSTER   LIAM NEESON   NATASHA RICHARDSON

"NELL"

RICHARD LIBERTINI

Music by MARK ISHAM   Costume Designer SUSAN LYALL   Film Editor JIM CLARK   Production Designer JON HUTMAN

Director of Photography DANTE SPINOTTI, A.I.C.   Co-Producer GRAHAM PLACE

Based on the Play "Idioglossia" by MARK HANDLEY   Screenplay by WILLIAM NICHOLSON And MARK HANDLEY

Produced by RENÉE MISSEL And JODIE FOSTER   Directed by MICHAEL APTED

SPECTRAL RECORDING
DOLBY. STEREO
DIGITAL

PANAVISION

© 1994 TWENTIETH CENTURY FOX

Nell

**A novel by Mary Ann Evans
based on the screenplay
by William Nicholson and Mark Handley**

BERKLEY BOOKS, NEW YORK

NELL

A Berkley Book / published by arrangement with
Twentieth Century Fox Licensing & Merchandising, a unit of Fox, Inc.

PRINTING HISTORY
Berkley edition / January 1995

All rights reserved.
TM & Copyright © 1994 by Twentieth Century Fox Film Corporation.
This book may not be reproduced in whole or in part,
by mimeograph or any other means, without permission.
For information address: The Berkley Publishing Group,
200 Madison Avenue, New York, New York 10016.

ISBN: 0-425-14533-6

BERKLEY®
Berkley Books are published by The Berkley Publishing Group,
200 Madison Avenue, New York, New York 10016.
BERKLEY and the "B" design
are trademarks belonging to Berkley Publishing Corporation.

PRINTED IN THE UNITED STATES OF AMERICA

10 9 8 7 6 5 4 3 2 1

PROLOGUE

Imagine, please, the face of a child.

She is in bed, composed for sleep but wakeful, a tingling sense of excitement and anticipation humming through her, keeping sleep at bay. She is a little girl, no more than four years of age, her heart-shaped face illuminated by the faint glow of the light in the hallway.

There are soft footsteps across the landing and the door opens, throwing a bar of bright light across the bedroom floor.

"Can't sleep?"

She shakes her head vigorously and smiles. They both know the reason for her restlessness.

The little girl's father seats himself on the bed, his weight firm and secure on the bedclothes, tightening the sheets, enclosing her tense and taut in the crisp linens. In that moment hers is a world of absolutes, the boundaries of that world are defined by the borders of her bed. Her imagination, however, nudges those confines as if anxious to wander beyond the room, traveling to a place far away, to another world.

"Excited about tomorrow?" he asks.

"Uh-huh." She nods solemnly. "I can't wait."

He is a powerfully built man in his early forties, tall and strong, with long legs and sturdy arms, big hands crossed with calluses. Yet there is a gentleness about him also: large, soft gray eyes and quiet, deliberate voice, a soft Irish lilt. He is dressed in an old checked shirt and blue jeans so old they had been blanched almost to match the color of his eyes. The effect is to make him look at once both careworn and boyish.

He smiles at his little daughter. "First you have to get some sleep. Settle down. Eyes closed."

The little girl snuggles down in the bed, burrowing into her pillows and closing her eyes tight. Her father smooths the sheets over her and then gently, softly, caresses her cheek. It was a gesture she had known and answered to since birth, a tender stroke that expressed a concentrated mixture of love and warmth, a simple signal that said so much.

"Love you," he whispered.

"I love you, Daddy." She looked up at him, the happiness glowing in her eyes.

"I said, eyes closed."

The little girl closes her eyes tight, her eyelids furled taut, as if that would make sleep come that much faster.

Her father pauses for a moment, then begins to speak. His voice is low and soothing, a rumbling chant, a rhythmic collection of words, flowing like soft water from a spring. To an outsider the father's refrain would appear to be nonsense, gibberish sounds strung together without meaning or reason.

"Lilten pogies, lilten dogies. Lilten sees . . ."

But the effect of the lyric is so familiar to the child that a little smile flits across her face when she hears it and almost at once her breathing softens and deepens, settling toward her slumbers.

"Lilten sees, lilten awes . . . lilten kine, lilten way. Lilten alo'lay . . ."

In those moments before sleep closes over her, the little girl's imagination floats free and drifts away, born aloft by the music of her father's words, spiraling up like a coil of sweet smoke and gliding off to a faraway place.

He sits for a long time on the edge of his daughter's bed, silent now, gazing at her with that scarcely containable love that a father feels for a child. He marvels at the commonplace details.

There had been a time when he noticed nothing and felt little besides pain. Of course, that had been before Nell.

He does not think of his own breathing or of the beating of his heart, but in his child these ordinary functions are phenomena that fill him with awe: the simple architecture of her face, a miracle; the smoothness of her skin, a wonder.

ONE

The wind off the lake was edged with the warmth of summer, but the tall, silent pines crowding the shore assert that this is a place of the winterlands. It lies high in the mountains, this lake, a pool of water cupped in the crater of a volcano older than ten thousand centuries. A narrow basin of old, cold, black water, ringed with high granite crags, bluffs pockmarked with crevasses and caves, the lake and the surroundings are barren, wild, remote. It is an isolated place, secretive, a place to hide.

Even the colors here are subdued, an unobtrusive palette of muted greens, grays, and pale purples, as if not wishing to call attention to the splendid mysteries of nature. The mountains are the splintered peaks of the Washington State Cascades, somber mauve against the cobalt-blue sky, cloud-ringed and enigmatic, like a secret in stone. The foothills are no less severe, crest upon crest of gray rock rising in steep steps from the shore of the lake. The conifers are a soft green and cast a shade as dark as the night. Only the sky, the big blue burning summer sky, is vibrant and vital.

There is a profound silence, broken only by the sound of the wind in the trees, the lapping of the water at the edge of the lake, and the rattle of pebbles on the shore. But beneath those muted sounds there is another sound, a sad, soft human sound. It is a woman's voice, muted and mournful.

"Lilten dogies," she sings, *"lilten dogies. Lilten sees . . . Lilten awes . . ."* The song is a dirge, laden with sadness and sorrow. *"Lilten kine, lilten way—"*

Someone lives here. Nestled in a narrow hollow a few hundred yards from the lake is a small, stout log cabin, the boards grayed by age and extremes of weather. A porch of uneven planks encircles the cabin and two windows look toward the lake; a brick chimney climbs one side. It is a plain but sturdy structure sitting on firm foundations. Strong winds might buffet it and the cruel snows of winter might bury it, but this simple house will always stand. The building is overgrown with lichens and moss, so covered, in fact, that it seems as if the building grew out of the forest itself rather than having been constructed by human hands. Close by the cabin, a short timber jetty thrusts out into the lake.

The sound comes from within. The voice falters and the words break off, as if the singer is too overcome to continue. Then another attempt. *"Lilten alo'lay . . ."* Then the slow decline into incoherent grief. *"Aiee m-mou . . ."*

It is a chilling animal sound, a wail of inconsolable anguish and deep fear. The shriek seems to hang in the air for a moment, silencing the wind and water, as if the land itself is listening, stilled by the penetrating grief.

For a long while, silence reigns. Then, far off, comes another sound, a sound more at odds with the surroundings than the chant of mourning. It begins as a distant but intrusive buzz, an angry, unfriendly sound. Then, as it draws nearer, it becomes more distinct and louder, throatier and deep. It is the growl of an engine.

In an instant the motorcycle bursts from the tree line and flashes into view. Rocketing along the shore, the engine screaming, the powerful bike seems like an infernal machine designed to chew up the peace, tranquility, and beauty of the scene. And the rider is oblivious to his sudden and abrupt act of desecration.

This blunt intrusion of a screaming piece of late twentieth-century technology serves to underscore the remote and solitary nature of the place. On this crowded planet there can't be many places like this remaining. There is no sign that the modern world has intruded—no cables for telephones, no TV aerials, no parked cars, not even the most rudimentary roadway.

But the rider noticed none of this. His name is Billy Fisher, a local boy, a wild, unthinking young man, whose deficiencies of character place him somewhere between thug and hoodlum. He is eighteen years old, no helmet of course, his long hair streaming out behind him. Over dirty blue jeans he wore a sleeveless leather vest that showed his tightly muscled arms and stomach.

Poorly educated and marginally employed, Billy Fisher's eyes were closed to any kind of beauty and his pleasures were simple ones: drinking beer, raising hell, getting into fights, playing pool, lifting weights, and pushing his dirt bike over difficult, wild terrain like this. To pay for these pursuits he took those jobs that came his way, the steadiest being his monthly delivery of groceries out here in the wilds.

Billy brought the bike to a halt in a shower of gravel and dirt, directly in front of the cabin. He cut the howling engine, slipped off the saddle, and busied himself with the carton of provisions strapped to the pillion seat. After the din of the motorcycle engine the silence seemed all the more profound and the sudden sound from the house all the more eerie.

"Aiee m-mou . . . m-mou . . ."

Billy Fisher heard the wail and froze. For a moment he thought it was an animal—the woods were filled with bear and birds—but even he could tell that the cry did not have the urgency of a cry of pain. This was an expressive, human sound, filled with longing and heart-ache.

He swallowed hard and mopped the sudden sweat from his brow and then hefted the box of groceries on his broad shoulders, walking cautiously toward the cabin. A door slammed and Billy jumped. But it was only the wind, banging the old screen door.

Fisher was spooked. He stopped at the base of the ramshackle steps, the hair on the back of his thick neck tingling. Something was wrong. "Deliver this shit and get the hell out of here," he mumbled. He climbed the first three steps. "Miz Kellty?"

There was no answer from within the cabin. Billy Fisher hated his monthly visits to the cabin. The ride out was always lots of fun, but he was frightened and repelled by crazy old Mrs. Kellty, the reclusive woman who chose to live in this remote place. There was something wrong with her too—Billy wasn't quite sure what, he had the youth's aversion to old age and illness—but her right side was stiff and unnatural, her speech horribly slurred and difficult to understand. Worst of all were her wild, staring blue eyes, eyes that watched him closely, warily, as if she suspected that the delivery boy was up to no good. There was never a tip, either.

He trudged up the steps of the house and pushed into the kitchen, slamming the groceries down on the table, hoping that the sound would announce his presence. "Miz Kellty? Got your groceries here." His eyes darted

8

around the kitchen, but he looked without interest. He'd seen it all before.

The low-ceilinged room was dominated by a large, cast-iron wood-burning cookstove, an old-fashioned pot-bellied lump of black iron, a fire burning within day and night, from one end of the year to the other. The other appliances were just as antiquated. There was a brass-bound oak ice chest, a tall hoosier cupboard with screened cabinets, and a big tin drum for flour. There was no running water, so no sink. Instead there was a gray tin basin and several large water jugs. The room was orderly and swept clean, but to Billy Fisher the simple kitchen was depressing and impoverished.

He shook his head in wonderment that anyone would choose to live so simply and with so few creature comforts.

"Crazy old bat," he whispered aloud.

There was still no sign of the old lady and the house was eerily quiet. The door to the interior of the house was slightly ajar. Gingerly Billy peered around it, squinting in the gloom, trying to make out the details of the room.

As his eyes adjusted to the dim light, he made out a rickety iron bedstead, a tall standing mirror, a hard, ladderback chair. A faint, musty smell seemed to hang in the room and Billy Fisher crinkled his nose in disgust. It was the smell of carbolic soap and old clothes, an old lady smell.

"Ugh," he said.

Billy took a step or two into the room. The body of Mrs. Kellty was lying on the floor. For a moment all he could do was stare. The body was laid out as if in a funeral home, the frail old body neatly composed for death. She wore a pair of stout, well-worn leather laced-up boots, a long gray frock, and a threadbare quilted jacket. Her old hands were laid across each other on her thin chest, the skin almost translucent, but mottled with liverish age spots and the cross-hatchings of deep blue veins.

Mrs. Kellty's lined old face was sunken, the cheeks slack and drawn, the thin lips almost bloodless. But, for a moment, Billy thought that the eyes of the old lady were wide open, staring at nothing but the timbers of the ceiling. But they were weird eyes, stranger even than the crazy look in the blue eyes that Billy knew so well; these were bright yellow and ringed with a stark white. It took him a second to realize that they weren't her eyes at all, but flowers. Someone had laid two daisies in the hollow eye sockets, white petals surrounding bright gold centers.

"Jesus Christ!" yelped Billy. Unable to tear his own eyes from the bizarre sight he backed toward the door, feeling his way behind him as he went.

Then a great bolt of fear surged through him and he turned and ran. He blundered through the kitchen and fell off the porch, racing for his motorcycle.

The engine caught on the first kick and roared into life, but Billy, in his haste to be away, almost stripped the gears, thrashing the machine into a hard turn. The bike screamed as he gunned the engine and ripped up the slope in a cloud of dust and pine needles. In a few seconds he was gone, the bike howling away, silence returning to the clearing as the dust began to settle.

Then the wail, the human wail, returned. *"Ai-eee m-mou m-mou . . ."*

TWO

Overweight, oxlike Calvin Hannick sat in a battered old armchair planted in front of his run-down trailer home like a shrub. His ham fist was wrapped around a can of beer and a cigarette hung from his fat mouth. From under thick brows he stared in sullen silence, looking at nothing and trying as best he could not to listen to his wife. From inside the trailer the TV blared, ignored.

Lorene Hannick, equally obese, sat in her own armchair. She did not have a beer or a cigarette, but she did have a gruesome trail of blood running down her fat cheeks. Jerome Lovell—Dr. Jerome Lovell—was bent over her, diligently cleaning the cut. The wound was not deep, but any scalp laceration would bleed profusely, and although no stitches were needed Lorene would end up with a very nasty purplish bruise for a week or two.

This was not the first time he had been called out here to patch up a Hannick—for her part, Lorene often gave as good as she got and had been known to bash her husband with whatever weighty object just might be at hand. Jerry Lovell was getting a little tired of ministering to this constantly bickering couple.

"Lorene, Calvin," he said wearily. "This kind of thing has to stop. One of you is going to kill the other."

"Kill himself, more like it," harrumphed Lorene. "That's what I tell him."

"Shuttup," countered her husband.

"I tell him you smoke too much," said Lorene. Her voice was a peculiar combination, both monotonous and grating at the same time. Jerry Lovell wondered how long he would be able to stand it. "I tell him you smoke too much and one day it's gonna kill you. That's all I said."

"And I say, says who?" said Calvin.

"I say, the surgeon general."

Calvin sucked the last smoke out of his cigarette and shot the butt into the road. "Who the fuck is the fucking surgeon general?"

"I say the surgeon general's not some dumb fuck like you, that's who he is. So he hits me."

Lovell pressed down a bandage over the wound and then straightened. "What did you hit her with, Cal?"

Calvin Hannick shrugged. "Picture."

"Wedding picture."

Lovell glanced into the trailer. Lying in front of the bellowing television was a photograph, fragments of glass scattered around on the stained shag carpet. The picture showed Lorene and Calvin, a quarter of a century earlier and half the size of the mountains of flesh they were today.

Lovell sighed. "You want to take it easy, Cal. You could have taken her eye out with that."

"Tell her to watch her fucking mouth," said Hannick. He pulled a crumpled pack of menthols from the breast pocket of his shirt and prepared to light up.

"And she's right, you should watch the smoking." You didn't have to be a doctor to see that between the excessive weight and the heavy smoking, there was sure to be a heart attack in Calvin Hannick's future.

"Yeah, yeah . . ." he grumbled. "Big fucking deal. I been smoking all my life. No problem yet."

Suddenly Lorene Hannick was on her feet, peering into the road. "What the hell is *he* doing here. I never asked for no sheriff."

Lovell glanced over his shoulder. The blue police cruiser of the two sheriff pulled up in front of the trailer.

Lorene was a trembling mound of indignation. "You leave him alone, Sheriff Petersen," she screeched. "He didn't do nothing." She touched the wound on the side of her face. "Well, not much, anyway."

Sheriff Todd Petersen raised his hands in a gesture of peace, as if trying to stop the noise with his bare hands. The policeman was a weary-looking man in his fifties, tired, it seemed, of dealing with people like Calvin and Lorene Hannick. But there were other, more personal demons he had to contend with, more serious battles than anything the Hannicks could concoct.

"Slow down, Lorene," said Petersen. "Relax. I didn't come out here for Calvin. I came for the doctor, okay?"

Mollified, Lorene Hannick lowered herself back into her armchair. "Oh," she said. "Sorry 'bout that."

"No harm done," said Sheriff Petersen. "Come on, Doc."

Richfield, Washington, was a tiny hamlet high in the Wenatchee branch of the Cascade Mountains, lying between the Cedar and Snoqualmie rivers. The names of the towns in the area—Startup, Goldbar, Index, and even Richfield itself—marked this as gold-mining country, settled by prospectors and later exploited by timber concerns. But with the demise of those environmentally unfriendly activities, the town had declined. Now Richfield got by on some seasonal tourism, but the primary employers were the ski resorts of Stevens Pass and Alpental, where Richfielders found steady, if low-paying, jobs as chambermaids and maintenance staff.

The population was small and law-abiding and Todd Petersen had little to do besides arbitrate domestic disputes, such as those that erupted from time to time among Richfield citizens like Calvin and Lorene Hannick, breaking up the occasional fight at the town's only bar, and enforcing the speed limit on County Road 971. He couldn't remember the last time his revolver had left its holster.

Petersen drove out of town, along a highway that was walled with thick stands of pine trees. They crowded the road and filtered the bright light, the car passing through bands of darkness and light, as if through a natural strobe.

"Billy Fisher found her," said Petersen. "He delivers groceries out there."

All the residents of Richfield knew something about the strange old lady who lived out by the lake, but few people had ever seen her.

"The woman in gray?" Lovell asked. "Is it true she always wore gray?"

Petersen nodded. "Yeah. The hermit. She was a strange old bird. Talked funny." Petersen screwed up the left side of his face, his lips tight and drawn. "Kind of like—durr yurr mmm . . . Like that."

"Stroke, probably. Only one side of her face was working. Nerve damage. You try talking out of one side of your face. Sounds like she did pretty well."

Petersen sighed. "I guess. She lived her own life. Can't blame a person for that." He swung the car off the highway and onto an old logging road, a dusty dirt track that was heavily overgrown from lack of use.

"Ever been out here?"

Jerry Lovell shook his head. "Never. I didn't know there were any folk living this far out."

"There aren't. Only Ma Kellty."

The car bumped over the track, slithered down the slope to the lake, and turned onto the shore, the wheels spinning in the gravel.

"Next time remind me to bring the Jeep."

Lovell was not paying attention. The lake, the hills, the forest—the whole scene was one of such compelling beauty that he could only stare in awe. He was not a native, had only lived in Richfield for a few years, and the magnificence of the scenery never failed to impress him. When he was up here, in the middle of the great wilderness, cities and city life felt far away and alien, an unnatural way of life.

The police car came to a halt in the level clearing in front of the Kellty house. Petersen got out of the car and walked briskly toward the cabin, then stopped and looked back. Dr. Lovell was standing still, examining the clearing, the house, the lake, and the mountains beyond.

Petersen laughed and shook his head. "You want to take photographs?"

"It's beautiful," said Lovell solemnly. "Don't you think it's beautiful?"

"Too many trees." In contrast to Lovell, Petersen had grown up and spent his entire life in this country and it had long ago ceased to impress him. He had no desire to move from his hometown, but unlike the outsiders Petersen did not get soft and misty-eyed every time he saw an evergreen or barn owl.

"What's the matter?" Lovell asked. "You don't like trees?"

Petersen looked around. "Not this many," he said with a wry grin. "Makes me feel outnumbered." He started toward the house. "C'mon, let's get this over with."

Jerry Lovell was no less fascinated by the interior of

the Kellty house. He stood in the kitchen, as if in a museum, riveted by every simple detail of the old woman's life. To Billy Fisher the primitiveness of Mrs. Kellty's life had deserved only scorn or, at best, a sort of grudging pity; to Lovell it was something to be admired, respected for its single-minded devotion to simplicity. Even those few imports from the modern world, her groceries, were old-fashioned. They stood in a row on the worn kitchen table: a box of oatmeal, dried beans, flour, baking powder, a carton of milk. The box they came in stowed away under the table, as if for future use.

Lovell touched the kerosene lantern hanging from the ceiling and set it swinging. "No electricity. No phone. No running water."

"Yeah," said Petersen. "Crazy, isn't it?"

"You think?"

"I try not to." He walked through the kitchen and into the bedroom and knelt by the body. In Billy Fisher's garbled, fear-struck account of finding the corpse he had mentioned something about flowers, but there was no sign of them now. To Petersen it seemed obvious that the death of the old lady was as simple as her life had been.

"How about that?" he said, shaking his head slowly. "Laid herself down, folded her hands, and died." He looked over his shoulder at Lovell. "Ever seen that before, Doc?"

Lovell had a wide experience of death, of course, and while he never became inured to it, he tried to force himself to look at it dispassionately, with the critical eye of a technician. Most deaths were an indignity, a final insult visited on a body that had been tortured in life. People died in pain and torment, consumed by disease, stricken with a final infirmity.

Doctors couldn't help but codify and classify death, assigning weight and value to each kind of demise, yet none, least of all Lovell, could escape the fact that the

16

battle against death could never be won, not in the long run. He had witnessed violent death, sudden death, long anguished death. But the good death, the happy death, the joyful death that theologians wrote about, was, in Lovell's experience, largely myth. However, as he examined the remains of Mrs. Kellty, he was forced to conclude that if there was such a thing as a peaceful death, this was it.

He could not establish cause of death from his cursory examination of Kellty's head, heart, and lungs, but he could make an educated guess. It was probably the simplicity of the old lady's life that had, in the end, killed her. Years of hard work in all kinds of weather, chopping wood, drawing water from the lake, would take its toll. Mrs. Kellty was probably always cold in the winter, malnourished too, when Billy Fisher failed to make it through the snow and ice with her provisions. In addition, she had probably not had any medical care in two, possibly three decades, a lack of attention exacerbated and complicated by the long-term debilitation of a stroke. The old woman's frail body had just worn out.

Lovell placed her somewhere in her middle sixties, though she looked far older. An autopsy would show this to be an old-fashioned death, uncomplicated by modern cancers and heart disease, by the stresses and complexity of contemporary life. This was a nineteenth-century death, a demise brought on by the exhaustion that claimed pioneer women. Mrs. Kellty had worked herself to death.

"Any idea how long she's been here?" Petersen's voice brought Lovell back to the present.

"Not long," he said. "The weather is warm enough that we'd know if she'd been dead longer than a day."

"Anything I should be concerned about? No signs of foul play, suicide, anything like that?"

Lovell shook his head. "Not that I can see. Like you

17

said . . . She just lay down and died." He paused a moment, as if uncertain about something. He ran his eye over the corpse one more time, as if double-checking.

"What?" asked Petersen. "What's up?"

Dr. Lovell shrugged and shook his head. "Nothing really, it's just a little strange that her hands didn't move during final necrosis. There really *is* something called a death throe, you know."

"I didn't."

"Well, there is. And there's a death rattle too."

"That I knew. But there wouldn't have been anyone within ten miles who would have heard it."

Lovell looked around the bare room. "She lived here all alone? No one could have composed the body?"

Petersen shook his head. "All by herself out here. Not a soul for miles. That's what hermits do, Lovell. Live alone. Die alone."

THREE

It took a long time for Todd Petersen to get hold of the
county ambulance on the radio in his cruiser and even
longer for that ungainly vehicle to make the trip up from
Monroe, the nearest big town and the county seat.

Lovell didn't mind the wait, happy to wander the
property examining the few outdoor artifacts—an ax
stuck in a tree-stump chopping block, a rusty reservoir
for kerosene, a waterlogged rowboat half submerged in
the lake—with the interest and intensity of an anthro-
pologist studying a remote and mysterious people. His
short tour of the grounds completed, he settled on the
edge of the jetty and admired the view, periodically
closing his eyes and turning his face to the midsummer
sun.

Seated there, the wind riffling his brown hair, his long
legs dangling over the cool blue water, Lovell appeared
to be a man with few cares. Little was known about him
in Richfield, save for the fact that he was a doctor, trained
in the northeast, who had come to the town only a few

years before to join the small practice of his partner, Amy Blanchard, a woman who had long been sole physician to the town. The locals assumed he was just another of those refugees from big city life who chose to forgo the money and prestige—or the action—of an urban career in return for the peace and quiet of small-town life. They were only partially correct.

By the time the ambulance had bumped over the difficult ground and the body removed, Todd Petersen was finishing his final check of the premises. It was late afternoon now and the small rooms of the cabin were suffused in a delicate amber glow, sunlight strained through the flimsy muslin curtains pinned to the window frames. Before leaving the bedroom, he paused and stood still in the middle of the room, as if trying to sense something he could not see. Throughout the day he had been possessed by an odd feeling, a curious sensation that although this silent house contained few objects and was empty of people, it felt occupied, as if somewhere in the house a soul still lived.

Petersen shook his head, amused by his own credulousness. "Crazy," he said and went outside to begin the paperwork, the bureaucratic process that would bring the sad but uneventful life of a mad old woman to its close. As he emerged from the house, Lovell walked back down the jetty to join him.

"So who gets this place?"

"Why? You want it?" Todd Petersen smiled slowly. "I saw you sitting out there. Bet you were wondering what it would be like to live out here. Commune with nature, right?"

"Maybe."

"You're welcome to it," said Petersen, heading for the police cruiser. "But it's too quiet for me. I like the bright lights of downtown Richfield."

Lovell laughed. "I know. They can be mighty seductive."

"Right," said Petersen slowly. He swung himself behind the wheel of the car and pulled his report book from behind the visor. He clicked his ballpoint pen and began making notes. Lovell shaded his eyes against the setting sun and looked back toward the house. Just as the sheriff had felt . . . something in the house, something had been bothering him, a nagging suspicion that something was out of place here.

"Billy Fisher found her when he delivered the groceries this morning?"

Petersen didn't look up from his report. "That's right."

"The groceries were unpacked."

This time Petersen did look up. "What's that?"

"I'll be right back."

That was it, of course. Lovell knew Billy Fisher—he had stitched him up after a bar fight hadn't gone his way—and he knew that the young man would not have troubled himself to unpack his delivery. Lovell suspected that helping others, even an old and isolated woman, was not high on Billy's list of personal priorities.

One of the cartons of milk had been opened. Lovell picked it up and weighed it in his hand, swirling the liquid to see how much was missing. No more than a mouthful. He sniffed. The milk was still sweet and fresh, a few beads of condensation still clinging to the plastic.

He opened the door to the bedroom and stepped into the nimbus of golden light that bathed the room. It was all as they had discovered it. The iron bedstead, the tall mirror, the hard chair, the amber curtain glowing . . .

There was a pattern of ridges and hollows worn into the timbers of the floor and he knelt to feel the smooth contours.

Then, from above, a sound. It was the tiniest sound, a faint squeak, the involuntary cry of fear strangled in the

21

throat. For a moment he thought it must be a mouse or a bat, but in the mirror, angled a few degrees toward the ceiling, he caught the slightest flicker of movement, something faint and indistinct, like the darkness of a shadow moving over the walls. But as he searched the mirror, the shadows in the rafters began to take form, the varying degrees of darkness slowly melding together. There was something up there.

Lovell slowly raised his head and looked up. There was something, a creature, an animal clinging to the roof beam, fear pressed it flat, pushing the body into the dark corner where the wall met the beam. At first the soft light coupled with the dark shadows seemed to melt the creature into the shapes of the room, but as Lovell stared the form became clearer.

A girl, or perhaps a young woman, it was hard to say. Her head was twisted back at an acute, awkward angle, huge eyes, gray-blue in that light, the eyes of a nocturnal animal, stared at him unblinking. Her hair was white-blond and close-cropped. Her face was white, bled of color, the skin stretched over her skinny, angular limbs almost translucent. She was dressed in nothing more than a pale, thin shift. Her feet were bare.

Lovell could feel the fear in the room, like the sudden, unexpected confrontation between man and animal. He stayed very still, too surprised to react and afraid that any sudden movements would startle her.

Keeping his eyes locked on hers, he spoke softly, cautiously, "It's okay. I won't hurt you."

There was no response from above. The huge eyes continued to stare without blinking, her body was still coiled, tense like a blade of sprung steel, making herself as small as possible. Carefully, deliberately, he raised his hand, open-palmed, toward her, as if to help her down from her precarious perch.

This brought a response. A warning hiss snaked from

her pursed lips, the noise growing louder as Lovell reached for her. The admonition changed in tone and intensity the closer he came, opening up, rising into her throat until it was deep canine growl.

"It's okay . . . okay . . ." Lovell spoke to her as if comforting a frightened child. "Easy now . . ."

When Lovell stood upright, the woman erupted, exploding into yelps of terror, gut-wrenching screams that filled the room, backing Lovell away. As she shrieked, her hands came out like claws, beating and tearing at herself. It was a terrifying and pitiful sight—the fear that possessed her seemed to make her want to rip out her own heart.

"Jesus!" He stepped toward her and the screaming redoubled. Her hands slapped at her head, flailing at her cheeks and temples as if trying to hammer herself into unconsciousness.

"Stop it!"

The answer was a horrible, bloodcurdling howl, a scream of affliction and agony, that ran across his nerves like a fret saw. Lovell stumbled out of the room, back into the kitchen, just as Petersen burst through the front door.

"What the hell is going on?" He pushed into the bedroom and the screams intensified.

Lovell yanked him out of the bedroom. "Leave her," he ordered. "She's scared."

"*She's* scared? Holy shit!"

"Outside! Outside!"

The two men stumbled out onto the porch, the screaming behind them unabated. Then the intensity dropped to a low yowl, as if having driven off her attackers she was warning them not to return.

Petersen and Lovell stared at each other, sharing their astonishment.

"Good God!" Petersen said, panting as if out of breath. "What the *hell* was that?"

"You ever heard of anyone else living out here?"

The policeman shook his head emphatically. "Never. Who is she? What do we do?"

"Okay," said Lovell. "Let's take this one step at a time." He turned back toward the house. "Stay here."

"What are you going to do?"

"Talk to her," Lovell called over his shoulder. "If I can."

"Be my guest," said Petersen, doing his best to calm his hammering heart.

Lovell crept into the house and stopped at the door to the bedroom, listening intently. The screaming had ceased, but he could tell that the woman was still agitated. He could hear shallow, rapid breathing interspersed with the sound of fast, pattering footsteps. It sounded as if she was racing around the room, circling the perimeter, on guard against the hated intruders.

Then she spoke . . . or, at least, she converted her ability to give voice to her alarm, changing her screams into something that sounded like speech and had the form of language. But it wasn't like anything Lovell had ever heard before.

"Doana Nell yow, law, kine'ey, kine'ey law, doana Nell yow."

Her voice was low, but the words were hurried and driven, as if she was urging herself to be resolute, to find the courage to protect herself against the interlopers. The tone suggested to Lovell that her words were a mixture of pep talk and diatribe. *"Smi'eva'dur, hai! Hai! Smi'eva'dur, zzzslit! Zzzzslit!"*

The *hai! hai!* and *zzzslit!* were uttered with a startling ferocity, as if they were vicious threats. Then the agitated pacing began again, the woman circling the room. Lovell could only guess at the turmoil she was going through.

The death of Mrs. Kellty, followed by this sudden, terrifying invasion of the house by two strangers, must have filled her with nothing short of abject terror. Lovell's heart went out to this poor, panic-stricken woman and he was filled with the need to calm her, to make her understand that she was safe.

He put his mouth close to the door and spoke softly. "Please," he begged. "*Please* don't be afraid."

"*Hai!*" The footsteps stopped abruptly. As he listened he could imagine her jumping like a frightened cat, crouching low as her frantic, frenzied breathing began to work itself up into anguished, high-pitched cries.

"Okay," he said. "Okay. I'm going. It's okay." He backed away from the door, but he didn't leave the building. He settled on his haunches and listened to the confused, disquieting sounds on the other side of the door. After a moment, the woman began to speak again, her voice filled with fear.

"*Doana Nell yow, law, kine'ey kiney law, kine'ey, kine'ey . . .*"

Jerry Lovell listened and rubbed his chin absentmindedly, listening to the skein of apprehensive words being unspooled in the room beyond. It was a language, a language *she* understood and used to inspire confidence. It was a support mechanism, an important part of her personal makeup. Lovell shook his head and silently cursed himself for not having paid more attention in those clinical and behavioral psych classes he had been forced to take in medical school.

He glanced toward the front door of the house, looking through the kitchen. From his position, low to the floor, Lovell noticed something that neither he nor Petersen had noticed earlier in the day. There was a shelf under the kitchen table, set back and under the top, a crude hidden compartment. A folder lay on the shelf, fat with yellowed

25

pieces of paper and a black-bound, well-thumbed book. Lovell knew at once that the book had to be a Bible.

The woman's breathing had calmed somewhat and her frightened speech had given way to a new sound, a low humming, a soothing murmur that followed a narrow range of notes, climbing and then falling. Lovell could not discern the meaning—was it a soothing melody, meant to calm her, or a piece of heartfelt threnody, sung in lamentation? The sound was nothing like he had ever heard before, at once both haunting and reassuring.

Lovell reached for the papers hidden under the kitchen table. The folder contained a sheaf of legal papers: land deeds, letters from bankers, a considerable correspondence from a lawyer in Tacoma. All of the letters and documents were addressed to Miss Violet Kellty and dated from the year 1960. Scanning them quickly, Lovell learned that the late *Miss* Kellty owned three parcels of land on the lake, free and clear, and possessed an annuity, a sum that might have been adequate three decades ago, but now must have decreased in payment considerably. This trove of information explained a great deal, but Lovell could see no clue there as to the identity of the woman in the adjoining room.

The humming was more intense now, filled with a sadness that seemed to come straight from the soul. The lilting chant rose and fell with the constancy of breathing, filling the air, then dying away, then coming back even and regular.

The Bible yielded only a single document, but one as interesting as all the rest put together. It was written in a large, unsteady hand, the kind of handwriting that was common among stroke victims, forced to write with the wrong hand.

The Lord led you here
strangr. Gard my Nell

Good child. The
Lord care you.

Lovell read the words a dozen times, amazed by them, as if he had found a message in a bottle, a call from a long lost mariner on a desert island. He rested his head against the door of the room and listened to the purring hum. This was Nell.

Four

"She's her daughter," said Lovell.

Petersen looked puzzled. "Who? Ma Kellty? I never heard she had any daughter."

Lovell placed the folder of legal documents, the Bible, and the sad little document on the hood of the cruiser. "Nell," he said. "Her name is Nell."

Quickly Petersen spread out the papers and began reading intently. He whistled and shook his head. "See this? That crazy old woman owned half this forest."

"And now Nell does."

Petersen smiled crookedly. "Well, unless she wants to sell, I don't think you'll be moving out here after all."

"I guess not," Lovell said with a laugh. "But I don't get it. What kind of deal is this? The first person who finds her is supposed to look after her?"

"That means you, Jerry."

"Oh, sure. Just what I need . . ."

Petersen waved Mrs. Kellty's note under Lovell's nose. " 'The Lord led you here,' he said. "There you go."

"You led me here."

"You want the Lord to care for you or not?" Petersen couldn't help laughing.

"Look," Lovell protested. "If I wanted to share my life with a crazy woman, I'd still be married and living in Philadelphia."

Petersen shook his head slowly, as if not quite able to believe that all this was happening. "Did you get anything out of her? I heard a lot of noise, but it didn't make any sense to me. Gibberish, I guess."

Lovell shook his head. "No. She talked all right. Trouble is, she didn't say anything in English."

"So what *does* she talk?"

"No language I ever heard."

Petersen sighed heavily. "You know, this started out as just a plain old normal Tuesday. First Ma Kellty pops off and now this . . . this . . . Well, I don't know what the hell to call it."

"Nell," corrected Lovell.

"Yeah. Her." The policeman stared up at the cabin. It was quiet now, no sign that there was anyone within. "What do we do? We can't just leave her here."

"We can't? She's been here a long time. At least, I guess she has. She's scared—terrified, probably—but when she found her mother dead she had the presence of mind to lay out the body. Sometime during the day she helped herself to some milk. While we were right outside here."

Petersen folded his arms across his chest and looked quizzically at Lovell. "You're saying we should just leave her here. Just walk away and forget about it."

"No. Of course not. But I don't see that this is police business."

"Well . . ." Petersen kicked at the soft soil under his

boots. "Somebody should be notified. Social Services or APS. Somebody like that."

Lovell nodded and began gathering up the papers scattered on the hood. "She doesn't need a social worker," he said. "She needs a padded cell. That is one seriously disturbed lady."

"That sounds more like your territory than mine," said Petersen.

"Thanks."

"The Lord led you here, stranger," said Petersen, chuckling.

"Then I guess I'll have to take care of it." Lovell was surprising himself, a little amazed that in a few short minutes he found he had developed a proprietary interest in the strange woman in the cabin. Having seen the unknowing terror in those blue eyes and having heard her suffering, he knew he had to step in and protect her, to shield her from the world, just as her mother had done for so long. It was a crucial decision, but one he made on the spur of the moment.

If Petersen realized the import of this decision he gave no sign. He merely nodded. "I'd appreciate that. I got my hands real full right now."

Both men knew that he wasn't talking about a sudden crime wave in sleepy Richfield, the late Violet Kellty, or even the sudden discovery of her mysterious daughter. Todd Petersen had troubles at home, troubles he tried to keep there, but in that he was not always successful.

Petersen slipped in behind the wheel of the car and fired up the engine while Lovell took one long last look at the cabin. The house was still, calm now, but he couldn't help but wonder if Nell was watching. He sensed that she was. What would she do next? Would she wait for the car to pull away and then run, hiding out, burying herself in the forest, or would she stay close to the only home she had ever known?

Silently he prayed that she chose to stay put. No matter how well one knew the woods, the wilderness could be an unforgiving place. From what he could see of her, Nell looked thin, frail, probably undernourished. He doubted that she could withstand the rigors of the wild for very long.

"Jerry," said Petersen. "I gotta get going . . ."

"Yeah. Sorry."

As the car crawled out of the clearing, Lovell turned to the driver. "What do you say, Todd? Let's keep this to ourselves. We don't want half of the whole county out here."

Petersen nodded. "I have to file a report. After that, she's yours." He smiled wearily. "And good luck to you."

FIVE

Twice in the next two days Lovell had returned to the isolated cabin to see Nell. The first time he knocked and entered, as if he was doing nothing more unusual than making a neighborly visit. But the cabin was empty and still, silent in that way that says that it has been uninhabited for hours.

His disappointment at not finding her was offset by a single, simple observation. The groceries had been put away in the kitchen cabinets and partly consumed. That told him that she was still close to home and he was relieved to find that she had not taken to the forest. Lovell had left some fresh milk and another carton of oatmeal on the kitchen table, a calling card to let her know he had been there, a peace offering that he hoped told her that he meant no harm.

The second visit was early on the morning of the next day. He had parked his Jeep on the roadway and had hiked through the damp timberland, approaching the cabin stealthily, hoping to catch sight of her without revealing his presence. He had settled in a thicket of trees, like a hunter in a blind, and had watched and waited, scanning the area through his field glasses. The sun rose above the sharp horizon and dried the dripping undergrowth and for hours he had nothing to show for his vigilance: there was no sign of her, no sound, no footfall, no twitch of the amber-tinted curtains.

Lovell was in an agony of indecision. He needed to know that Nell was all right, safe in her seclusion. Yet he did not want to approach the cabin again for fear of driving her off, the way an animal will abandon a nest or den fouled by the touch of an outsider.

Then, around noon, his watchfulness was rewarded. At first he was not even sure he heard it, maybe it was nothing more than a trick of the wind in the trees.

Then it became clearer, Nell's voice, singing in Nell's language. Nell's song. *"Lilten pogies, lilten dogies, lilten sees, lilten awes, lilten kine, lilten way, lilten alo'lay . . ."* The sad, soft cadences drifted across the clearing like the voice of a songbird.

Lovell was surprised at the depth of his relief. He listened until Nell finished and then he left for Seattle.

Having fled the city once and for all, Jerry Lovell was loath to return, even if only for a visit. However, he knew his strengths as a doctor and he knew his weaknesses as well; Nell's case was beyond the purview of his medical specialties and even his basic training and he knew he needed help.

And he hated asking for it. He had not been able to shake the disquieting hunch that he had possessed since that first day—Nell needed to be protected, like an animal in the wild, and the more people knew about her, the more likely she was to come to some harm.

During the long drive through the mountains to the city, Jerry Lovell, country doctor, did his best to metamorphose into Dr. Jerome Lovell, serious medical practitioner. He stopped at a gas station between Bellevue and Seattle and changed into a jacket and tie and attempted to put a shine on his scuffed shoes.

Over a lunch he scarcely noticed, he read and then reread the report he had written, a summary of the events of the last few days coupled with his own medical observations. Lovell was not happy with his work. It seemed thin and haphazard and his own awkward forays into psychological jargon seemed inexpert and forced. More than once he winced in embarrassment, dismayed at his presumption and the glaring lacunae in his knowledge.

He felt like a fraud.

Some thought had gone into the design of the psychiatric wing of the Washington State Medical Facility. From the outside, Lovell was pleased to see that in contrast to most state asylums, this one was not a red brick gothic horror, the kind of place one need only look at to imagine the screams of inmates long dead. It was a modern, well-tended hospital, the building itself a long, low, artfully designed structure, constructed largely of glass, meant to bring natural light to the interior, an antidote to the somber Seattle weather.

The instant Lovell walked through the front door, though, he realized that he had been misled by appearance, for no matter how skillful the design, it could not fully mask the depressing nature of these places. The hospital was clean, efficiently run, and the patients appeared to be well cared for. And yet the halls and lounges reeked of that dispiriting sense of finality, that this was a dumping ground for broken souls.

Waiting for his appointment, Jerry Lovell watched the shuffling parade of patients, men and women of all ages wandering the corridors, their eyes dull, their limbs lolling. A handful were slumped in front of a bellowing television, six sets of vacant stares. Throughout the building Lovell could feel the aimlessness, the sense that lives were just trickling away.

Professor Alexander Paley was the kind of man who prided himself on his firm handshake. A hearty, bluff man in his early sixties, he carried himself with an air of authority that was meant to reassure but which Lovell found irritating. He had studied with professors like Paley in medical school and knew the type well—that slight smirk, the knowing glance, the feeling that when he called you "doctor" he was thinking "sonny."

There was no polite conversation. Paley apologized, told Lovell he was running late, and suggested that they walk together to his next appointment. It took a second or two for Lovell to realize that they would not be having a confidential chat in the professor's office, but a hurried conversation as they charged through the halls.

"You have a report, I trust?" The two men were striding down a corridor, Paley waving and mouthing greetings to every doctor he passed.

"Yes." Lovell noticed that the professor didn't seem to see the patients.

Paley had that knack for quick reading; scarcely glancing at the two typed pages, he seemed to get it all at once. "Screams. Beats herself. Climbs walls." He shot a sidelong glance at Lovell and raised an eyebrow, like a professor grilling a graduate student in senior seminar.

"She acts like she has no experience of other people," said Lovell hurriedly, as if anxious to please. "There's no record of her birth. My guess is that the mother kept her hidden."

Paley grunted and pulled another sentence out of the report. "Speaks an unknown language? Just what does that mean, Dr. Lovell?"

"The mother was paralysed down one side. Stroke.

36

Possibly even a series of them. The daughter presumably picked up the speech distortions."

"Speech distortion isn't an unknown language," said Paley with a frown, as if that grad student had let him down.

"I know that. But there's more there than just a speech impediment. I'm sure of it."

Paley came to an abrupt halt, stopping before an open door. Inside, grouped around a conference table, a number of doctors waited for Paley. But the professor ignored them, turning the full power of his attention on Lovell, fixing him with a friendly but somehow unnerving look. He was silent for a long time, like a judge weighing his sentence.

Finally: "Okay, Dr. Lovell. You interest me. I'd like to put someone on to this case."

Lovell neither expected nor wanted this kind of help. As far as he was concerned, there already *was* someone on the case. He shook his head curtly. "I'm only asking for a psychological assessment, Professor. I'd like to know what I'm dealing with. Then—well, if I can deal with it, I will."

The professor half turned toward the seminar room. "She's your patient?"

"Of course. I want to do what's best for her." *I* want to do what's best for her, he thought.

"So do we all." Professor Paley shook Lovell's hand and flashed him a paternal smile. "That's the first principle of medicine. The patient's needs are always more important than our own." He swept into the room and closed the door, leaving Lovell alone in the corridor.

"I knew that," he said. "Thanks."

In the cold, hard shine of the fluorescent light, the look of exhaustion and disillusionment set in the mother's features seemed as if they could never be erased, just as the irritating sixty-cycle hum from the fixture seemed to underscore the irreversible nature of her son's condition. They sat side by side at the table, mother and son isolated together in the examination room, she staring wanly at the floor, he slowly, methodically, rocking in the plastic chair, punctuating his swaying by banging his forehead on the tabletop.

The mother did not wince. She seemed a long way past dismay, exhausted by the exertion of emotion, angry at herself that the ability to feel love or pity for her child was being leached out of her.

She scrabbled in her purse and pulled out a small plastic box. "You want a mint?" she asked.

The boy looked at her blankly and then did his best to repeat his mother's words, but all he could manage was a confused jumble of syllables. The doctors had a word for this: echolalia. The doctors had a lot of words. Big words that masked nothing, proved nothing, cured nothing.

She uncurled his fingers and dropped the white dot in his fist. He stared at it a moment and then recommenced his rocking and head banging. His inability to place the mint on his tongue irritated the woman and she half turned in her chair, as if she didn't want to see him.

"You want to hurt yourself," she snapped, "go ahead. Hurt yourself. I don't know what you want."

Autosomal recessive inheritance, the doctors called it. The mother called it her fault.

Abruptly her son stopped and looked at her. A crooked smile crossed his lips and for a moment his clouded eyes seemed to shine. In a moment her exasperation flew from her and she saw the little boy, *her* little boy, her baby, in the pure light of love.

"Oh, honey." The mother threw her arms around his neck and squeezed him. But the moment had passed. He squirmed out of her grasp and began to rock again.

Tears came to her eyes. "Please, honey. The doctor'll be here soon. She'll give you something. She'll make you feel better. You'll see. Please, honey."

The examination room was a cold, charmless box, three walls painted an institutional gray, the fourth covered almost in its entirety by a large mirror. Behind that mirror, sitting in the darkened observation room, was Paula Olsen. She watched the sad little tableau through the one-way glass dispassionately, taking exact and detailed notes on the behavior of mother and child.

Olsen was in her late twenties, a year away from her doctorate and becoming a little bored with the scene framed in the mirror. The boy was over ten years old and his development was at a standstill. From a purely clinical point of view his case was declining in interest every day, the annals of clinical psych were crammed with case studies like this one, and while Paula felt for the child and the predicament of the mother, she couldn't see the point in more observation. She tried, at all costs, to keep her personal feelings from clouding her professional judgment.

Yet she continued to take notes, because that was what she was trained to do. Might as well finish out the session before she recommended that this case be back-burnered permanently.

Paula Olsen was very bright and very good-looking. She had prominent, well-formed cheekbones, a wide, slightly voluptuous mouth, and a cascade of soft auburn hair. Her eyes were large and had a slightly dreamy cast to them, a softness that stood in contrast to the sharpness of her mind and tongue. She wore no makeup, the look that says "take me the way you find me."

The door to the observation room opened behind her and Professor Paley stole in next to her.

"Okay to interrupt?"

Paula was glad to have any distraction from the dispiriting scene in the mirror.

"I have something for you." Paley put Lovell's report down in front of her, centering it in the pool of light on the writing table.

"What is it?"

"Read it," said Paley. "I think you'll find it very interesting. It has all the makings of a classic."

Paula read the two pages quickly, feeling a bubble of excitement rising within her as she took in the information. Now *this* was interesting.

"Who found her?" she asked, not taking her eyes off the page. "This—Lovell."

"That's right."

The boy had stopped banging his head and was now sitting motionless looking utterly lost, withdrawing into his own world. His mother stroked his hands gently and hummed in his ear, the sound of her voice coming through the speaker tinny and distorted.

"Who is he?" Paula Olsen asked.

"He's one of the local doctors up there," said Professor Paley dismissively. "But he's out of his league on this one. At least he had the sense to come to us."

Olsen looked her mentor square in the eye. "You think she could be a wild child?"

"Perhaps something far more rare. A wild adult." Paley smiled his slow, knowing smile and folded his arms across his chest. "That would be quite something, wouldn't it?"

Paula nodded, thinking of the research possibilities. "Yes, it would."

"Like to look into it?"

"I would."

"Then go ahead," said Paley, as if bestowing Nell on her, a generous gift from master to apprentice.

SIX

Lovell got back to Richfield early in the evening, but he had no desire to return to the empty house he rented on the south side of town. Instead, he drove to his office on Main Street, pulling his Jeep gingerly into his parking space, narrowly missing a young drunk slumped at the curb. Lovell's office adjoined Richfield's principal bar, a raunchy beer-and-a-shot place called Frank's Bar. By seven o'clock in the evening the serious drinking was well under way and the place was packed. The air pulsed with the thump of music from the jukebox, punctuated by the occasional raucous shout from one of the patrons jammed three deep at the bar. Fights were a frequent sport and pastime at Frank's and Jerry Lovell couldn't count the number of times he had been called in to sew up a split lip or tape up a set of cracked ribs.

Occasionally, the proprietor of one of Main Street's more respectable businesses would start a petition to get rid of the bar, fed up with the morning ritual of sweeping up broken glass or hosing pools of vomit off the sidewalk. Lovell and his partner, Dr. Amy Blanchard, would sign dutifully, but Todd Petersen would not.

"It keeps all the trouble in one place," he would say. "Why spread it out all over town?" Besides, he liked Frank and did not think a man should be deprived of a legal living, no matter how disreputable. Somehow Frank's always managed to dodge eviction.

Lovell scarcely glanced at Frank's or at the drunk sprawled in the gutter, hurrying into his office. The secretary-receptionist had already gone home, leaving him a stack of messages, some over two days old. He riffled through them quickly, hoping that no emergencies had arisen during his absence—since the discovery of Nell he had been neglecting his practice shamefully.

"What happened to you?" Amy Blanchard stood in the doorway of his office, fixing him with a very stern gaze.

Lovell smiled sheepishly. "Hi, Amy. Did you cover for me?"

"Sure," she said with a shrug. "What else do I have to do all day but cover for the junior partner?"

Blanchard was almost always infinitely even-tempered, but this evening a look of distinct irritation was stamped on her lined—and usually friendly—features. A tall, silver-haired woman in her late fifties, Amy Blanchard was a dedicated physician and a native Richfielder. It was entirely due to her that Lovell had moved to the little town in the first place.

She had heard through the extended physicians' grapevine that Jerry Lovell, a rising young oncologist, had abruptly resigned from his hospital appointment in Seattle and was looking for a less stress-filled position. Blanchard had solicited him with all the perseverance of a college coach recruiting a hot high school quarterback, extolling the natural beauty of the Cascades and the friendliness of the Richfielders, not to mention emphasizing the lack of pressure in her little country practice.

It was only after he had moved there he realized that Amy Blanchard had stretched the truth a bit. He couldn't argue with the splendors of the countryside, but while most of the inhabitants of the town were friendly, there was an abundance of surly types like Calvin Hannick and Billy Fisher. As for the practice, he learned something he should have known already: there is no such thing as a job in the medical profession that does not carry with it a measure of anxiety. But by the time all of this had sunk in, it was too late for him to back out. Besides, he had become attached to Blanchard and to the town. Whenever he contemplated leaving, he thought of Blanchard or one of his patients and decided to stick it out a little longer—and now, with the discovery of Nell, departure was unthinkable.

"Jerry, where the hell have you been?" Blanchard demanded. "I answered three of your calls today."

"Anything serious?"

Blanchard shook her head. "No," she grumbled, "but everything takes time, you know."

"Sorry, Dr. Blanchard," he said meekly. Then he smiled. "Amy, you're going to forgive me when you hear what I found."

Amy looked skeptical. "What did you find, Jerry? Sasquatch?"

"No," he said evenly. "But close . . . A wild woman. Snarls like an animal. She speaks some kind of private language. Climbs walls."

"Tell me she's an alcoholic and abuses her kids and you're talking about my average patient," she said with a thin smile.

"You know, you really did feed me a crock when you told me how great this practice was."

"I had to. I was desperate."

"Well, this makes it all worth it," said Lovell. "I mean it, Amy. She's very, very unusual."

43

"I'll bet." The look of incredulity had not left Amy's face. "And just where did you find this wonder?"

"Way out, by the lake."

Now Amy looked surprised. "Violet Kellty's place? I heard the poor old soul had died . . ."

"You know her?"

Amy laughed and shook her head. "No, Jerry. I didn't know her. Nobody knew her. She wasn't from here. I was away at medical school . . . must have been about 1960, maybe '61. When I came back someone told me that a hermit had moved in out there. High country seems to draw strange people. People who want to be left alone."

"People like me?"

"No. You're in the wrong business for peace and quiet. You know that."

"You never met her? Never spoke to her? Anything you can tell me would be valuable."

Blanchard thought for a moment. "Violet Kellty had at least one stroke, you know. I heard about it from Mickey Tyler—he was Billy Fisher about fifteen years ago—so I went out there. She was so weak, just lying in that old bed, nothing but skin and bones. She should have been in a hospital but she wouldn't hear of it. She was furious that I had come; she damn near tried to run me off the property with a shotgun—no mean feat for a stroke victim."

"I'll say."

Blanchard laughed ruefully and shook her head. "She was hardy stock. Kept that gun right next to her bed like Mammy Yoakum. I wouldn't be surprised if she smoked a corncob and cooked up white lightning in a still."

"Well . . . I don't think so," said Lovell, thinking of the well-worn Bible. "She seemed to have a pretty wide religious streak."

"See. You know more about her than I do."

"But what happened, back when she had the stroke. What did you do?"

Amy Blanchard shrugged. "What could I do? I left her some strophanthin and got out of there, but I kept sending some out with Mickey. I could never figure out how she got through serious thrombosis without care."

"Well, she *had* care. Her daughter. Nell."

"A daughter!" Blanchard was completely taken aback. "Jerry, it's not possible. I can't believe it."

"Believe it. I may be one of the two people besides her mother to see her with my own eyes."

"A feral adult?"

"That's right. She is domesticated in the purest sense of the word—she lives in a house. She wears clothes. She cooks her food. But she is almost completely unacclimatized to society. She lives with minimal comprehension of life beyond her"—Jerry shrugged—"I guess you'd have to call it her territory."

"Which she goes out and marks with her scent, right?" said Amy cynically.

"See. That's exactly what I'm afraid of. A lot of people are going to want to put her in a cage and feed her peanuts."

"I'm sorry . . . What do you want to do with her?"

"I don't know." He thought for a moment or two. "I was down in Seattle today, talking to the experts." He smiled wryly at the word. "I can't do all that much until I get some kind of evaluation." Lovell stood and patted his pants, making sure he had his car keys. "First, I guess I'd like to see what she's like when she isn't scared out of her mind."

Lovell drove off the main road and along the overgrown logging track that led down to the lakeshore. He was going to drive closer than he had that morning, but well before reaching the Kellty cabin he killed the headlights and rolled slowly through the brush, coming to a halt near to where he had been earlier that day.

A light was burning within the house, filling the rooms with the soft golden glow thrown by a kerosene lantern. Through his binoculars, Lovell caught sight of a slip of a figure, a sudden blur of movement as Nell passed one of the saffron-colored windows. He was staring intently through his field glasses, but for a long, long time there was no movement within. Lovell lowered the binoculars and sat still, his eyes fixed on the house, silently urging her back to the window.

Then, as if she had heard his mute entreaties, she reappeared at the window, gazing out into the night as if seeing something imprinted on the darkness. She did not look at Lovell and seemed unaware that she was being watched. He raised his field glasses again and studied her face, amazed at the change in her. Devoid of fear, Nell's face was calm, infused with a smooth serenity that said that she was at peace with herself and her surroundings.

She was also beautiful. Years of isolation and hard-scrabble living had not taken any toll on her face. Her blue eyes were sparkling and clear. Privation had thinned her, but even from a distance Lovell could see that her skin was smooth and glowed with health, her hair was soft and shining. Absentmindedly, as if she was unaware that she was actually doing it, Nell raised the fingers of her hand to her face and stroked her own cheek. It was a slow and tender gesture and she trembled slightly, as if deriving great comfort from the simple action.

"This is no wild animal," Lovell whispered. All of a sudden he felt like a voyeur, a peeping tom intruding on a scene not meant for his eyes.

Nell did not see the Jeep, because before her eyes, the Jeep was not there. Lovell wasn't there, not part of the scene or reality. Nell had gazed through her wide, unseeing eyes, looking intently not at the present, but into the past.

Out there, in the night, Nell could see her memories. The jetty, reaching out into the lake, was a dark bar across the glimmer of reflected moonlight and the wind carried with it the lilting sound of the laughter of children. Nell could see shapes at the end of the pier, bodies formed from a trick of the light and the fading shadows. They were little girls, twin girls, seven years old, identical: the same braided blond hair, the same long loose white frocks, the same slender bare legs.

As they stood facing each other, they played a private game, laughing as they played. This was their own secret ritual, intimate, comforting, familiar, a rite played out to the counterpoint of a whispered nonsense chant.

"Chicka, chicka," they murmured. *"Chickabee . . ."*

The twins stood, hands before them, fingers raised, their palms pressed together. They raised their hands, up, up, until their arms were straight up over their heads.

"Thee'n me an' me'n thee," they chanted, their soft voices hushed and tranquil. Their palms separated and they clasped their own hands together and lowered them over each other's heads.

"Ressa, ressa, ressa me . . ."

As the two loops forms by their arms dropped down over each other's shoulders and backs, they inclined their heads, their brows touched.

"Chicka, chickabee . . ."

At this final, still point, their bodies outlined in profile by the gleam of the water, this ritual had become an image, a potent portrait of trust, sharing, of mutual support. They were linked, but not in a full embrace, neither clinging nor possessive.

They were standing close together at the far end of the jetty, one arm around each other's waist. Their other

47

arms rose up and out giving them the appearance of being a single child, with two outstretched arms. They began to spin slowly, turning in a full circle, then, suddenly, they fell backward into the darkness, toward the water. Never bending nor separating as they toppled, it was an act of pure trust, pure letting go, as if they were doing nothing more than falling down on a soft bed. There was a faint splash and then they were gone.

Lovell neither saw nor heard any of it.

Nell had the faintest smile on her face, remembering.

SEVEN

In due course, Todd Petersen reported the lonely death of Violet Kellty to the Department of Social Services in the state capital, Olympia, and in return the authorities there faxed him the information they had on her. There wasn't much.

Two sheets of paper scrolled out of the fax machine. Petersen cut them and showed them to Jerry Lovell. One was a birth certificate, the other a social security data card. "This is it. Her whole life, officially. You have any idea how hard it is *not* to generate paperwork in this day and age? By the time you hit thirty you've got a file on you six inches thick."

"Big brother," said Lovell.

Todd Petersen shook his head and laughed sardonically. "There's nothing sinister about it. It's just that these days you can't help but leave a paper trail. Unless you're a hermit like old Ma Kellty. Seems her taxes and such were filed by that law firm down in Tacoma. I spoke to them yesterday. No one there had ever met her or knew anything about her. The one partner who *did* know her died in 1969. Violet Kellty was just about as lone as a soul can get in this world."

"Except she wasn't," protested Lovell.

"Officially, that creature doesn't exist," said Petersen.

"But she *does* exist."

Petersen smiled his slow, ironic smile. "If she's not in the files, Doctor, she does not draw breath. Not according to the great state of Washington, she doesn't."

"That's probably not such a bad thing. Wish they didn't know about me." He thought a moment. "Well, we know who the mother was, how about the father. If we could trace him, maybe there's a chance he'd—"

"The law firm sent me this . . ." said Petersen, interrupting and turning serious.

It was a fax copy of a newspaper clipping. Lovell winced when he read the headline: DEVOUT CHURCHGOER RAPED. There was a date scribbled in the margin, 10/31/65. Lovell read the article quickly.

"Jeez, the guy was not apprehended—but that doesn't stop them from printing her name *and* address. No wonder she left and hid herself way the hell up here. She must have been scared to death. Terrified." According to the brief details provided by the newspaper, it seemed that Violet Kellty had lived an unexceptional life up to the terrible day in October of 1959. She was a cashier in a drugstore, active in a local pentecostal church, and lived alone.

The fragments of the puzzle that made up this odd life were beginning to fit together. A single, random act of violence and Violet Kellty's world had been shattered. Stigmatized by a sexual assault that had been splashed in the newspapers, shame probably caused her to separate from her mainstay, her church—or worse, the church had driven her out.

To find herself pregnant by her rapist must have been

the final blow, the event that pushed her into the life of a recluse. She delivered the child alone, in the woods, and it was a measure of the sort of woman she was that she had chosen to love and raise the child—a child who must have reminded her of her trauma every time she looked at her. And yet Lovell knew that Violet had loved her daughter. The words Violet Kellty had scrawled in the Bible came back to him: *Gard my Nell Good child* . . .

"This story gets more and more amazing," Lovell said. "Mind if I keep this?"

"Be my guest," said Petersen. The phone rang and he answered it on the first ring. He listened for a moment, his features darkening. "Where is she now? Okay . . . I'll come right over. Thanks, Frank. I appreciate your trouble."

Instinctively Lovell knew what the trouble was.

"I have to go," said Petersen quietly.

"Your wife?"

The sheriff nodded. "Yeah," he said with a sigh. "Mary."

"Is there anything I can do?"

Petersen shot Lovell a look, a look that seemed to verge on the edge of despair. He shrugged. "What can anyone do?" he asked.

As Todd Petersen slowly walked down Main Street, he could see a small knot of bystanders gathered on the sidewalk in front of Frank's Bar. It was the usual crowd, midafternoon drinkers and the layabouts on Main Street, just standing there, slack-jawed and gaping with the pitiless curiosity of the dull-witted. Petersen felt a stab of anger when he saw them, that these people were getting a little thrill, titillated by the public sufferings of another. They could shake their heads and say that poor old Todd Petersen sure had his hands full with that wife of his . . . Phony sorrow that masked a sense of smug self-satisfaction.

Mary Petersen sat in the gutter, dressed in nothing more than a flimsy cotton nightgown, the pattern faint, as if it had been washed out. Her bare feet were in the dust. She was hunched over, her lank brown hair obscuring her face, her thin shoulders shaking as she sobbed.

Frank, the bar owner, had laid a beefy arm across her shoulders trying to comfort her, but she cried on, oblivious to the man's feeble attempts at solace.

Todd Petersen elbowed his way through the crowd. "Show's over, folks. Clear the sidewalk."

"I heard this hollerin', Todd," said Frank, straightening up. "Came out, there she was."

"It's okay, Frank. Thanks." Petersen crouched down next to his wife and took her in his arms, a weary, protective love. She seemed to release herself into his embrace, clinging to him as if he alone could provide safeguard. She dissolved into the embrace and slowly her sobbing began to subside.

"Okay, honey, okay," he said quietly, smoothing her hair. "I'm here now. You're okay now . . . Let's go home."

The crowd was drifting away now, leaving only Lovell watching the sad little scene. Mary Petersen was his patient, but her depression was so profound that there was little he could do for her. He felt sick at heart and helpless when he saw her, disturbed that there wasn't more he could do. Other doctors would have prescribed a powerful cocktail of tranquilizers and antidepressants, doses of diazepam and librium, but Lovell knew that the doses would have to be large, so large that they would do nothing for Mary except to drug her into near insensibility. The drugs would make her docile and easy to control, but would do nothing to affect a cure.

52

"You want me to come around later?" Lovell asked quietly.

"I guess so," said Peterson, guiding her into his car. "If you think it will do any good." He sounded like a man resigned to the weight of his burden.

"I'll be in my office," said Lovell. "Call me if you need me."

Petersen nodded. "Will do," he said, knowing that he wouldn't. Sometimes the hopelessness of his wife's condition threatened to overwhelm him, but he tried to banish the feeling. He had no alternative but to be strong for her. He could not allow himself to falter.

Lovell watched the Petersens drive away, then turned back toward his office. There was a car, a red MGB convertible, parked in the space at his front door, a young woman sitting behind the wheel. Lovell had the sense that having witnessed the entire scene between Todd and Mary Petersen, she was now turning her attention to him.

"This your car?" Lovell asked.

"Yes."

"You maintain it yourself?" He ran an eye over the sleek lines of the little sports car.

It seemed an odd question and she hesitated slightly before she answered. "Yes."

"It's in my space."

Her eyes flicked toward the brass plate on the front door of the office, then back at him. "You Dr. Lovell?"

"That's me."

"Is that woman your patient?" They both glanced at the departing police car, now rolling slowly away down Main Street.

Lovell nodded. "Yes. She is."

"What medication is she on?"

"Who wants to know?"

The woman slipped out of the car, extending a hand.

"I'm Paula Olsen, Medical Psychology Unit, Seattle General."

"Professor Paley sent you?"

Olsen nodded. "That's right."

"Okay," he said. "I don't do drugs. That answer your question?"

"It tells me a lot," said Paula.

The two regarded each other with sidelong, inquiring glances, as if taking each other's measure. Lovell had to admit that Olsen was pretty—very pretty—but that was of no significance to him. It had taken only a few days for him to develop a fierce and jealous possessiveness over Nell and the sudden arrival of Paley's emissary did not please him. He had not wanted "someone put on the case," as Paley had suggested, and yet here someone was. She was a threat—to him, to his autonomy, and, ultimately, to Nell. All he had to do was determine how much of a threat and how difficult it would be to get rid of her.

For her part, Olsen was coolly sizing up Lovell. A physician who did not believe in drugs . . . that was a position that was becoming more and more popular these days and suggested that if nothing else, Lovell was keeping up with the latest trends in pharmacology—which was something, she supposed. However, he was the gatekeeper who stood between Olsen and her subject and, as such, would have to be won over . . . before he was discarded.

"Why are you here?" Lovell asked bluntly.

Olsen smiled. "You certainly know how to make a girl feel welcome . . . You asked for our help." She cocked an eyebrow at him. "Remember?"

"I *asked* for a psychological assessment," said Lovell. "That's all."

"I hope you weren't expecting anything in depth based on the two-page report you compiled," she said archly.

54

The suggestion that he was considerably out of his depth was unspoken but obvious. "To make any kind of educated evaluation of the subject would require some fieldwork. You must see that."

Lovell didn't like the tacit criticism, nor did he much care for the term "subject" in referring to Nell. But he had to admit that she did have a point.

"You want fieldwork?" he grumbled. "You've got it."

"This is pretty country," said Paula as Lovell guided his Jeep down the forest track toward Nell's cabin. They had just broken free of the dense tree line and had caught the first glimpse of the lake. The water shimmered in the late afternoon sun and the countryside seemed more welcoming than ever before.

"Pretty and remote," said Lovell with a nod. "No one is too likely to bother you out here."

"What was she hiding from?" Paula asked. "Why bury yourself like this?"

"Violet Kellty was raped."

Paula blinked hard. "That wasn't in your report."

"I just found out."

"Tell me about it." Paula Olsen slid a leatherbound notebook out of her backpack and attempted to take notes as the Jeep juddered along the track.

"1965. Violet Kellty is just forty years old. She's religious, unmarried. Probably a virgin. One night she's assaulted, robbed, raped . . . Just about as traumatic as it comes, I'd say."

Paula nodded. "And then some."

"The assault itself may have triggered a stroke. There's no way of knowing that now. She might even have been subject to a long series of recurrent thrombotic seizures. *Then* she discovers that she's pregnant. What would you do?"

Olsen scarcely considered the question. "Well, in 1965

abortion was more or less out of the question . . . Adoption, I guess."

Lovell nodded wearily. "Okay. Okay . . . I asked the wrong person. What would Violet Kellty do? She hides herself away from the world. She gives birth alone. Out here. The baby is never registered. Hides the child. Hides the shame. But she loves her and raises her as best she can. It's a pretty amazing story, don't you think?"

Paula Olsen had heard a lot of amazing stories. "That would make her twenty-nine," she said. "Nobody stays hidden that long."

"No?" Lovell looked around at the dense trees, the austere crags, and the sweep of the lake. "It's a big forest."

EIGHT

Lovell parked his Jeep closer to the cabin this time, drawing the vehicle almost up to the steps leading to the porch. He wanted to avoid taking Nell by surprise, to give her ample warning that they were coming.

"Does she come out of the cabin?" Olsen asked, taking in the scene.

"If she wants to. There's nothing to stop her."

"Then what makes you think she's been kept in isolation?"

"See for yourself," Lovell said, ushering her up the worn wooden steps.

Nell was waiting for them, standing in the doorway between the bedroom and the kitchen. She was hunched and tense, her back arched like a spooked cat, ready for flight. Her head was down and she glowered at them, eyes burning, a low and threatening growl emerging from deep in her throat. All color had drained from her face.

Lovell felt fear and pity at the same time, but Paula

Olsen was more businesslike, approaching carefully, her hands open wide to show that they were empty.

"Nell . . . ? I'm Paula Ols—"

The growl grew into a scream and Nell's screech filled the room, the sheer volume of frantic noise stopping Olsen dead in her tracks. But she did not give ground. She stood absolutely still, her eyes closed as if waiting out the storm of sound. Nell retreated into the bedroom, never taking her eyes off the interloper. She hardly glanced at Lovell, aware, it seemed, that Paula Olsen posed the greater peril. When the screaming died down slightly, Olsen tried again, placing one foot very carefully in front of the other, as if walking a tightrope across the Kellty kitchen.

"Nell?"

The single word set her off. Nell screamed— *"Hai! Hai!"* —then bolted into the bedroom, snarling and screeching. The sharp nails on her hands clawed at her face and chest and she scampered in a tight circle in one corner of the room. Every few seconds, she smashed her head against the stout timbers of the walls, each blow making the house shudder.

Lovell couldn't help himself. "Nell! Nell! Please stop it! Please!"

But his pleas seemed to make her redouble her fury. The screaming and snarling escalated and she raked her nails across the white skin of her thin chest, carving deep red welts.

"Be quiet!" snapped Olsen.

"She's going to kill herself!"

"You're just making things worse. Wait outside."

"But—"

Olsen spoke through clenched teeth. "I said, *wait outside.*"

The strength of Olsen's order and the intensity of Nell's distress drove Lovell out the door. He flung himself down the steps and tried not to listen to the impassioned screams from within. The woods seemed to ring with her anguish.

Then it stopped. The screams died away, replaced with the indignant *"Hai! Hai! Zzzslit!"* that he had heard before. Paula Olsen stood on the porch, unruffled and unperturbed by Nell's display of violent behavior. Without a word to Lovell, she took her notebook from the front seat of the Jeep and started writing. Her coldness, her business-as-usual manner, unnerved him.

"She's not like that when she's on her own," he said quietly. "Strangers scare her."

Olsen scarcely looked up from her writings. She glanced at him, then returned to the work at hand. "How do you know she's not like that when she's on her own?"

"I've been watching her."

This time, she stopped writing, put down her pen, and looked at him, a cool, appraising gaze. "You've been watching her?" she said evenly.

Lovell shrugged, unnerved a little by the impassive stare. "Someone's got to look after her. Don't you think?"

"And you're volunteering?"

"Maybe."

"Think you're up to it?" Paula Olsen glanced down at her notebook, as if she needed to refresh her memory.

"How do you mean?"

"I mean, she's manifesting some pretty extreme behavior, Dr. Lovell."

"I gathered."

"Taking care of her could turn out to be a full-time job, you know." She turned back to her notes.

Paula Olsen did not show it, but she was rather excited by Nell and her extreme behavior. Professor Paley may have been overstating things when he said that this case had all the makings of a classic, but there was a lot going here, plenty to interest a psychological clinician like Olsen. But Lovell had staked his claim and he was probably going to defend it—it didn't worry her much, not yet anyway—but there were ways of dislodging him if he chose not to go quietly.

"Have you seen enough?" asked Lovell. "Done enough fieldwork?" There was a little sneer behind the last word.

Olsen smiled to herself and shook her head slightly. No, she thought, he's not going to go quietly. Clearing a free path to Nell was going to require a little muscle and that meant bringing in the big guns, like Professor Paley. The professor was well entrenched in the medical and scientific community of the state and he had some valuable political contacts in Olympia. She doubted that a country doctor like Lovell would be able to prevail against the pressure that could be brought to bear.

But for the time being she wanted to know more and to avoid an outright breach. "Tell me," she asked. "Have you taken a blood sample?"

"No." It had never occurred to Lovell to take a blood sample. He shuddered to think how Nell would react to a pair of strangers sticking a needle in her arm.

Olsen fixed him with that cool, slightly mocking gaze again, as if she couldn't help but be amused by his amateurishness. "It is *usual* to try and find out what's wrong before trying to put it right, don't you think?"

"You're not trying to tell me that this"—he waved toward the cabin—"that this could be systemic, are you?" He laughed and shook his head. "Tell me you're joking."

"Could be anything," Olsen said with a shrug. "We can't rule out any cause for what's wrong with her."

"What's wrong is her mother died."

"Maybe."

Lovell felt himself growing angry. "What's wrong is

60

that her mother died and since then she hasn't had any peace from a bunch of outsiders she fears."

"Outsiders who spy on her?" She flashed him that venomous little smile again.

"She did not see me," Lovell insisted.

"Well . . . doesn't matter. But we *do* need a blood test." She closed the notebook with a sharp snap.

"Why?"

"Because I'd say that she is almost certainly mentally retarded."

"You would? That's a pretty hasty judgment, isn't it? Based on five minutes of screaming."

It was Paula Olsen's turn to get angry. "This is what I *do*, Dr. Lovell."

"And just what is that, Dr. Olsen? What is your specialty?"

"Autism and social deprivation," she said evenly. "And I'm not Dr. Olsen. I don't have my doctorate yet."

"Ohhh," said Lovell, nodding. "Now I get it. *That's* your doctorate." He pointed toward the house again. "Nell is your *thesis*."

"She could be part of it. It depends . . ."

"On what?"

"On her blood test."

"What is that going to tell you?"

Olsen sighed heavily. "If the cause of retardation is prenatal infection, childhood disease, or one of the metabolic disorders, a blood test will pick it up. And we can treat it. If it's parental abuse, schizophrenia, developmental aphasia, or autism, we go another way. You carry a blood kit in the Jeep?"

"Yes," said Lovell. But he didn't move.

"Let me guess," said Olsen. "You don't want to hurt her, do you?"

"I'd like to get her to trust me," said Lovell quietly.

61

"That doesn't seem to be unreasonable. She won't understand. If I hurt her . . ."

"Fine," Paula Olsen shot back. "You want me to bring in someone else to do the hurting?"

"I—" All Lovell could do was stare at this cool and brutal young woman. "You might kill her," he said.

"Don't be ridiculous."

"She could run."

"We'll find her."

Lovell swung around, his arms wide as if to embrace the entire green expanse surrounding them. "Out there?"

"She won't run."

"Well, what if she does?"

"We'll deal with it when it happens."

"Very convenient," Lovell snapped. "Besides, you've seen her. She's not going to just sit there and let me stick a needle in her."

"I'll hold her."

"Simple as that?"

Paula Olsen started back up the porch steps. "Yes. As simple as that," she called over her shoulder.

Nell seemed to sense that this onslaught was different from the others, that this time the intruders had something on their minds beyond mere observation. Her eyes grew wide when Lovell and Olsen stole her into the bedroom and she backed away from them slowly, her eyes flicking back and forth from Olsen to the fearsome-looking hypodermic needle Jerry Lovell held in one hand. She crouched down in a corner, folding herself into a tight ball, making herself as small as possible.

Lovell felt sick at heart and sick to his stomach, silently appalled at what he was about to do.

"Nell," he whispered, "it's all right, Nell. We want to help you. We have to do this to help you."

Nell whimpered and her breathing became short and

shallow. She closed her eyes, her whole face contorted, then banged her head sharply against the wall.

Lovell winced at the sound of impact and faltered. "Don't do that," he begged. "*Please* don't do that."

Nell opened her eyes and saw, horror-struck, how close they were, closer than any stranger had ever been before. Her reaction was instantaneous. She went straight to high-pitched terror, her screams as sharp as a blade, her arms flailing and tearing.

Lovell stopped, then backed off, horrified at the magnitude of her agony and torment.

Paula Olsen did the opposite. She darted forward and threw her arms around the screaming woman and held her close, embracing her. For a moment Nell screamed and struggled, then suddenly she went limp and silent. She was following the instinct of all wild creatures that find themselves in mortal danger: she was playing dead. Olsen did not relax her grip, but hugged her, feeling her hot skin and pulsing blood. Nell's chest heaved.

Lovell had not moved. He was rooted to the spot, staring, shocked by the sight. He realized that in a strange way he had come to accept Nell as a screaming, flailing animal. To see her surrender, to feign death, was even more astonishing.

Olsen, however, seemed intent only on seizing the moment. "Do it," she ordered.

Lovell seemed incapable of action. He took a single, uncertain step toward the two women, then stopped again.

Olsen's voice flared, low and insistent, angry. "Do it! Do it now!"

Her ire pushed him to action. He forced himself closer, pushing back the loose sleeve of Nell's linen jersey and exposing her skinny white arm. He had an alcohol-soaked cotton ball hidden in his left fist and he managed to swab it across the skin. The blue vein in the crook of her elbow stood out against her pale skin and he jabbed the needle into it, cringing as she flinched at the pain. Quickly he siphoned a long draft of blood. There were tears in his eyes.

Nell's howls followed them out of the house. But her voice had none of the urgency of the past; this sound was low and mournful, full of shock and self-pity, as if she had given up. She sounded as if she had been violated.

Lovell threw his black doctor's bag into the back of the Jeep and slammed the tailgate. He hated himself for what he had done and hated Paula Olsen for forcing him into it. He hated her smug, cocksure ways and her clinical lack of compassion. Most of all, he hated the air she had, the unspoken suggestion that they had done some good that day.

Without a word, Lovell got behind the wheel of the Jeep and started the engine.

"In my opinion," said Olsen, "she needs to be admitted to a psychiatric facility, where she can receive the professional care she needs."

Lovell didn't even look at her. "In my opinion, your opinion is a heap of shit."

His angry words did not even dent her professional reserve. "Do you get this emotionally involved with all your patients, Dr. Lovell?"

He slammed the car into gear and then turned to face her. This time it was Lovell who doled out the fixed, cold stare. "Yeah," he said gruffly. "I try."

Nine

The slow, outmoded computer in the Monroe Public Library considered Lovell's request for a long moment, as if the machine was of two minds about granting it. The public library in Richfield had closed years ago, a victim of a declining tax base and a general lack of interest, so Lovell had been forced to make the long drive down through the mountains to the library here in the county seat.

The computer decided to smile on his request. There were four books in the library dealing with feral children, the classic being Thierry Gineste's *Victor de l'Aveyron: Dernier Enfant Sauvage, Premier Enfant Fou.* Lovell did not understand enough French to read the entire book, but he could translate the title and it did not please him, neither did it support his point of view: *Victor of Aveyron, The Last Wild Child, The First Mad Child.*

Victor was probably the most feral child in history. Discovered in rural France in the eighteenth century, he was thought to have been raised in nature by wild beasts. Adopted by a local doctor who tried to domesticate him, Victor died a miserable death because, it was thought, his soul was stifled by the suffocating effects of civilization. Victor, *l'enfant sauvage*, became a symbol of the noble savage so revered by the rational philosophers of his time. It was now thought that Victor was severely retarded, a misunderstood case, who died of ineptitude and neglect.

Gineste's book could only support Paula Olsen's contention that Nell was a mental deficient who needed to be looked after by the state. Lovell put it aside.

More promising were the other three titles, Paul Massanet's *Bear Children, Monkey Children*, a study of feral children discovered in remote regions of India and other parts of the Far East. Two other books, though, really quickened his pulse: Stephen Renquist's *Language and Isolation* and Susan Curtiss's *Genie: A Psycholinguistic Study of a Modern Day Wild Child*.

Lovell found both books on the shelves, then settled in a corner to read them, taking copious notes as he went. Neither book provided him with a key to understanding Nell's language, but they did give him some insights into how she formed her speech, what thought processes were at work.

By the time the library closed for the day, Lovell had thirty pages of notes but also the discouraging sense that in terms of erudition, the opposition was light-years ahead of him. He had no doubt that Paula Olsen and Alexander Paley were well acquainted with the literature of feral children and they must know that most of the scholarship supported their contention that there was no such thing as a wild human, merely retarded ones whose development had been further impaired by an asocial and unorthodox rearing. It would take more than spending a few hours with the meager collection of books in a provincial library to fight them on the facts as established by years of learned research.

Lovell hardly noticed the scenery or the other cars on the road as he drove back to Richfield. He turned the problem around and around in his mind, trying to devise a strategy that would protect Nell. He felt as if he had taken over for Violet Kellty, as if he had been charged, somehow, with the task of sheltering Nell from the outside world and that he had to be as vigilant as her mother had been.

It was an unusual position for him. Lovell considered himself an activist, a hands-on doctor who sought to heal his patients of their ills, but now, with Nell, his was a conservative position, a defense of the status quo. Try as he might, he could not think of a reason for removing Nell from her natural habitat—she was happy in her isolation, far happier than she would be in a psychiatric hospital. Violet had seen to it that she would be taken care of financially, so her daughter would never need anyone or fail to have her simple requirements met.

However noble, however tidy it might be to try to draw her out, to "cure" her, he could not think of a better course than simply leaving her alone.

But the challenge was coming and he had to be ready to defend against it. Olsen and Paley would say that they knew best, that they alone could care for Nell, that she was a child in need of their help. His only hope was to prove them wrong, to show that Nell was her own woman, a figure functioning within her own society. He had to show that she wasn't a wild woman or an imbecile or even a case study, but a human being.

He drove straight through Richfield, not stopping at his office or home, going directly out to Nell's cabin. There was moonlight on the lake that still night, the only sound the gentle lapping of the waters on the shore. There were no lights showing in the house, no smoke in the chimney, yet he wasn't fearful this time, not worried that she had fled to the forest. Somehow he *knew* that she was still there, safe within the tumbledown little house.

Lovell liked being in this silent place, feeling small and undetectable under the great baldachin of stars and planets. He liked being near Nell.

He couldn't have said how much time passed as he sat there—a long time, long enough for him to detect a shift in the stars framed in the sun roof of his Jeep—but he wasn't concerned with time.

When Nell appeared on the porch of her house, he first thought it was a trick of the light, and he squinted in the darkness to convince himself that she was actually there. She did not look in his direction, unaware, perhaps, that he lurked there, watching for her.

Quickly and silently she crossed the clearing and walked to the end of the jetty, stopping at the farthest point and standing stock-still for a long moment.

Then Nell seemed to shiver, a quick corkscrew gesture of her slim shoulders, and she shrugged out of her dress, the thin material falling in a wrinkled pool at her bare feet. There she stood, naked and pencil-thin, her pale skin glowing in the moonlight.

Lovell heard his own breath catch in his throat and he stared, not daring to move, as if the slightest motion might catch her eye and startle her into flight. Seeing her like this, he realized that she was more beautiful and graceful than he had ever thought possible.

Nell raised her arms, lithe and willowy, then spun slowly around and fell backward into the water. There was a faint splash and then the black water closed over her. Lovell stared at the spot, marking it with his eyes, waiting, his heart pounding, for her to reappear. Moments lengthened into seconds and he felt a rising panic.

"Nell . . ." he whispered, trying to urge her out of the depths. His throat was dry and constricted and he found

68

himself fumbling with the door handle. "Nell, for God's sake!"

Then she burst to the surface. She was smiling, radiating happiness, water streaming from her face. Lovell saw her for a second only before she filled her lungs with cool air and dove again, slipping under the waves and swimming away, a naiad in the night.

Lovell awoke to the sound of the phone ringing. He opened his eyes and groggily reached for the telephone. He was in his own bed, in his own house. As he came awake he felt a dream slip away.

"Did I wake you up?" The voice on the other end of the line was Todd Petersen's.

"It's okay," said Lovell, rubbing his eyes. "I overslept." He glanced at the clock on his bedside table. It was after nine o'clock. At first he thought his dream had been of Nell, Nell swimming in the lake—then he realized that it had not been a dream. He *had* sat by the lake deep into the night, watching her cavort.

"You okay?" asked Petersen.

"Yeah . . . sure . . . What's doing, Todd?"

"Well, I'm sitting here with a care order. Just been issued. It's for Nell."

Lovell was fully awake now. While he had been musing under the moonlight the night before, Paula Olsen had been busy. "That fucking bitch," he yelled. "Olsen, right?"

"The same," said Todd Petersen. "And someone called Paley. Alexander Paley. Know him?"

"Yeah. I know him." Lovell turned on the speaker phone and vaulted out of bed, hurriedly pulling on a pair of blue jeans, then searching his dresser for a clean shirt.

"So," said Petersen. "What am I supposed to do with this thing?"

"Can you lose it or something?" Lovell buttoned his shirt quickly, then began hunting out his shoes.

Petersen laughed. "Lose it? No, I can't lose it. Jerry, it's a court order. I have to enforce it."

"I need a little time, Todd. Can you enforce it slowly. Drag your feet a little?"

There was a long pause. Then: "Well, I guess I can take my time."

"How long have I got?"

"I guess I can hold off until after lunch."

"Make it a long lunch."

"I'll try."

"And, Todd . . . Any idea where Don Fontana is?"

Petersen chuckled. "Well, I know he's not in his office. Not since the smallmouth season opened. If I were you I'd try the north fork of the Tolt."

Don Fontana was Richfield's only lawyer, another refugee from the big city who tried as best he could to keep his job from intruding on his leisure time. There was just enough legal business in the town to earn him a decent living, but the instant his work was done he fled his office for the fishing in the streams and rivers that crisscrossed the countryside.

Lovell found him up to his hips in water standing just upstream of a little set of rapids, a line from his fishing rod trailing in the water.

"Hey, Don," said Lovell, climbing out of his Jeep. "How come you're always fishing when I need a lawyer?"

Fontana never took his eyes off his line, watching the float bob in the fast water. "How come you're always bugging me when I'm fishing, Jerry?"

Lovell grinned. "Sorry 'bout that, Don. But I've got a little problem."

"I figured. People never come to me with good news."

"You should try being a doctor."

"I should try being retired," said Fontana, wading out of the stream. He sat down on the riverbank and unbuckled his waders, pulling them off with a wet splash. "What you got?"

"You heard about Violet Kellty."

"Uh-huh."

"Did you hear about her daughter?"

Fontana did a double take. *"Daughter?"*

Lovell nodded. He was pleased at Fontana's reaction—it meant that Nell's existence was still a secret—a valuable commodity in a small town like Richfield. "Seems she had a daughter. Delivered her all by herself and raised her out there in that cabin. We're guessing she's just about thirty years old, maybe twenty-nine. We're not sure."

"Incredible," said Fontana, shaking his head. "I've been hearing stories about Ma Kellty for as long as I've been up here. But I never heard anything like that."

"Stories? What stories?"

"The usual," the lawyer said with a slight shrug. "That she's a witch . . . that she's the bogey-lady. The kind of thing kids say. But nobody ever mentioned a daughter."

"Well, she's there. But there's a problem." Quickly Lovell explained his problem with Olsen and Paley, the court-issued care order, and his doubts about the wisdom of removing Nell from the only home she knew.

Fontana didn't much care for work, but he relished a good fight, particularly when the opponent was the state of Washington or a federal agency. He listened intently, but Lovell could see that he was already thinking, planning his strategy.

"The state would have grounds for removal on a strictly limited number of points," he said. "For instance, is her life in danger out there?"

Lovell thought of her effortless swimming in the dark

waters of the lake and then shook his head. "I don't see how."

"And she's not underage. You're sure of that?"

"Absolutely."

"How about her mental state?" Fontana asked. "Is she mentally underage?"

Lovell grimaced. This was a much trickier issue. "Well, there's no denying that her mental state is a little . . . unsettled. But that's to be expected. After all, she just lost her mother. That would be enough to disturb anyone, under any conditions."

Fontana nodded. "Sure."

"And added to that complete strangers keep on showing up and harassing her, naturally she's upset." He closed his eyes and saw again the fear and hatred in Nell's eyes as they tried to take her blood.

"But is she *competent*?"

"Maybe. Maybe not. That has not been established yet."

"And next of kin?"

Lovell shook his head. "None."

"Guardian?"

"None," said Lovell. "Don, Nell doesn't officially exist. Until a few days ago no one knew she was alive, except for Violet Kellty, of course."

"None of that matters," said Fontana with a chuckle. "That's the beauty of this."

"The beauty?"

"She's still got rights. You don't need a social security number for those. Is she capable of informed consent? That's the key."

"Informed consent?" Lovell thought for a moment. "In principle, I don't see why not. But I doubt if she'd understand what she was being asked."

"Why not?"

"Nell speaks her own language."

Fontana's eyes opened wide. "Her own language?"

Lovell nodded. "That's right."

"Wow . . . Her own language . . ." Fontana chewed his upper lip for a moment. "You know, that's not such a bad thing. The law is very clear on informed consent."

"What do you do now?" asked Lovell.

"Well, first thing we do is go to the office and do some work," said Fontana. He started gathering up his equipment, breaking down his fishing rod, and stowing it in its case. He sighed heavily. "No more fishing, though."

The small caravan of vehicles bumped along the track toward Nell's cabin, Paula Olsen leading the way. She was behind the wheel of her MG, heedless of the effect of the rough terrain on the delicate suspension of the sports car. Immediately behind her was Todd Petersen in his police cruiser. Bringing up the rear, making its second trip to the cabin in a week, was the ambulance from Monroe.

Olsen's car rounded a bend in the road and then came to a sharp halt, her path blocked. Angled across the path was Lovell's Jeep, Lovell and Fontana leading against it, as if on guard.

Paula Olsen shot the two men an angry glance as she got out of the car, but she didn't bother to speak to them.

"Sheriff," she said to Petersen, "would you deal with this, please."

Todd Petersen heaved himself out of his car and walked toward Lovell and Fontana, a piece of paper in his hand.

"The sheriff is carrying a duly-executed court order that requires us to take Nell into care," said Olsen.

Petersen shrugged apologetically. "Sorry, Jerry." He touched the brim of his hat. "Howdy, Don."

"How you doin', Todd?"

He proffered the piece of paper. "Sorry, but the lady is

73

telling the truth. She went down to Monroe and got herself a court order and it's up to me to enforce it. That's just the way it is."

"It's in Nell's own best interest," said Olsen sharply. She was tired of being treated like the villain in this little drama. If Lovell and Petersen couldn't see that Nell was desperately in need of help, then so be it. Nell's well-being was her only concern and the sooner the meddlers and amateurs got out of her way, the sooner Paula could get down to the serious business of helping Nell.

"Her own best interest?" said Lovell. "How do you know? Have you asked her?"

"Well, look," she said, feeling her small reserve of patience draining away. "You know that's impossible."

"Well, that's kind of a pity," said Lovell, a little smile playing across his features. "Because we went down to Monroe ourselves this morning and Don managed to get a court order of his own."

"Is that so? And what does yours say?"

Lovell took a deep breath. "It says that unless Nell gives her informed consent to being taken into your care, you are violating her rights. And if you do that, I'm going to sue you all the way to the Supreme Court. Show 'em, Don."

Don Fontana drew a piece of paper from a battered briefcase. "Here it is."

Todd Petersen did his best to hide his smile. Paula Olsen had no control over her own reaction to this development. Her cheeks flushed red and her eyes flashed angrily. "This is ridiculous. How can she give her informed consent? She's not capable of doing any such thing. She doesn't even speak English."

"Well," said Fontana slowly, "the law is quite clear, Miss . . ."

"Olsen."

"Olsen. If she doesn't speak English, she must give her

74

consent through an appropriate interpreter. It's as simple as that."

Olsen rolled her eyes and half turned as if ready to storm away. Then she stopped and stared the two men down. "This is crazy! What interpreter? There isn't anybody on earth who speaks her language. You know that, Lovell."

"Then I guess somebody's going to have to learn her language," he said.

Paula Olsen turned to Todd Petersen. "Sheriff, you've seen her. You have to know she isn't normal."

"Not being normal, that's no crime," said Petersen with a smirk. "Particularly not in this county."

"Now look, Sheriff," Olsen retorted angrily. "This is no joke."

"You're right, miss." Todd took off his hat, swept a hand through his hair. "And I know one thing . . . looks like we're *all* headed into court."

TEN

Small-time, small-town crimes were the norm in Judge Murray Hazan's county circuit court, but he was the sitting judge in Monroe, so Lovell and Olsen were forced to put the case before him. The judge was amenable to Don Fontana's suggestion that the hearings be closed and informal and he further agreed that the experts in the matter, rather than the lawyers, should argue the merits of their cases.

Paula Olsen was at her most controlled and judicious as she presented her case, as low-key as Lovell had ever seen her. Despite her decorous presentation, her argument was forceful, as well as reasoned, cogent, and persuasive.

"Dr. Lovell's view seems to be that this woman's natural habitat is a primitive cabin in the heart of the forest." Olsen paused and looked over her shoulder at Jerry Lovell, challenging him. "To put it plainly, he thinks she's Bambi. Her mother has just died and he has to protect her from the cruel hunters."

Lovell exhaled loudly, indignantly, and looked away. He knew that Olsen was not telling the truth, but he had to admit to himself that she was making her case well.

As if to confirm his feelings, Judge Hazan smiled benignly and nodded at her to continue.

"I take a different view," she said firmly. "I see a mature woman who has been robbed of half her life. I don't see why she should be kept as a pet in the forest to act out the sentimental dreams of a middle-aged hippie."

Even Don Fontana laughed, but Jerry Lovell felt his cheeks coloring. Her words stung, not just because he was embarrassed, but because somewhere in his heart he *did* doubt his own motives. Was his concern born of romantic fantasy or out of genuine desire to protect Nell from the interference of the outside world?

"Well," said Judge Hazan, still chuckling. "You made your case pretty forcefully, Ms. Olsen. Mr. Lovell?"

Jerry jumped to his feet. "Yes, Your Honor?"

"Why don't you say your piece?"

"Thank you." Lovell paused a moment to consult his notes. Where Paula Olsen had been restrained, he was more passionate, more fervent.

"Nell is not the first of her kind to be found," he said. "There was the German wolf boy. The Irish sheep boy. Kaspar Hauser. The Salzburg sow girl. The Indian panther-child. And the most famous of all, Victor, the *enfant sauvage* of Aveyron."

If Judge Hazan had heard of any of these famous cases, he gave no sign.

"Closer to home," said Lovell, "there was Edith of Ohio, and Genie, the closet child of Temple City, California."

It was Paula Olsen's turn to be impressed. It was plain that Lovell had done his homework.

"And all of these cases have one thing in common," he continued. "Be they in Europe in the eighteenth century, in the Far East, or here and now, in every single instance, their lives were destroyed. Destroyed by doctors and scientists who claimed to be helping them. We cannot allow that to happen again here. We cannot sit still and let them turn Nell into a guinea pig."

Olsen's self-control vanished. She was on her feet and shouting. "If she is ever to leave that cabin, she's going to need skills she does not presently possess."

"How do you know she wants to leave the cabin?" Lovell shot back. "Judge, Nell is perfectly happy in her environment. She doesn't want to be dragged out of it. Leave well enough alone."

"She's in prison," said Olsen angrily. "Don't you have any interest in setting her free?"

"Maybe she sees freedom differently. Maybe she doesn't *want* to be free. Not on your terms, anyway."

"Jesus!" Paula Olsen spun around, angry at herself for losing control of her argument.

Judge Hazan moved to calm both sides. "Okay, okay," he said. "I think I'm getting the picture here. There appears to be well-reasoned arguments on both sides . . ." The judge smiled slightly and peered over his glasses. "Not to mention a degree of fervor . . ."

"Judge Hazan—"

As Lovell began to speak, Don Fontana put a restraining hand on his arm. "Judge's turn, Jerry," he whispered.

Judge Hazan paused a moment before continuing. "I'm going to defer my decision for three months," he said. "And this time is to be used for the purposes of observation and assessment." He looked from Olsen to Lovell. "I hope that by the end of this period, the court will be better informed."

Failing, as it did, to designate one clear winner, Judge Hazan's solution pleased neither Jerry Lovell nor Paula Olsen. Yet it appeared for a day or two that Lovell had won the contest by default: Paula Olsen had walked out of the courtroom and without a word to anyone drove away, heading down Route Two, the road that led to Seattle.

Fontana and Lovell watched her go, waiting in silence until the taillights of her car disappeared around the corner before speaking, as if afraid that she could hear them.

"Think that's the last of her?" Fontana asked.

Lovell shook his head. "I don't know. I hope so."

"She seemed pretty fired up."

"I get the feeling she likes to get her way."

Fontana shrugged. "You know her better than I do. What are you going to do now?"

"I'm going to buy a tent," said Lovell.

Lovell had pitched his new tent unobtrusively between two trees near the edge of the lake, his only concession to comfort a canvas sunshade raised next to it. Nell did not appear to protest the arrival of her new neighbor and for most of the morning the clearing was still, disturbed only by the light summer breeze blowing off the lake. Then around noon, Lovell heard an unfamiliar sound, faint at first, but quickly growing louder. A minute or two passed before he could identify it—it was the low rumbling chug of a marine engine.

Lovell shaded his eyes against the sun and looked out into the lake where he saw—to his immense surprise— the boxy bulk of a houseboat plowing through the light chop of the water. The ungainly little craft was making for the clearing and he had no doubt who was at the wheel.

"You have *got* to be kidding," said Lovell with a slow shake of his head. "This is not happening."

There seemed to be no end to the ingenuity of Paula Olsen. Skillfully, she maneuvered the houseboat up to a mooring point not far from the jetty, and cut the engines. She emerged from the wheelhouse a moment later, dumped a sea anchor off the stern and then walked a spring line forward, dropped into the shallows, waded to shore and made the craft fast, hitching her line to the trunk of a stout pine. She dropped a gangplank from the bow and turned to Lovell. "Good morning." She had a triumphant little smile on her face, and that irked Lovell immensely.

"Permission to come aboard?" he asked, fighting down his irritation.

Olsen gave him a "suit yourself" shrug and vanished into the cabin. He stepped inside and looked around.

"You're planning on sleeping here?" asked Lovell. He had expected some sort of response from Paula Olsen, but nothing of this magnitude.

"That's the idea." She slid an armful of clothes into a dresser drawer. "I gather you are too." Olsen cocked a chin in the general direction of his tent.

Lovell ran an eye over the boxes of books and provisions. He had to admit that Paula's rig looked a lot more comfortable than his lowly pup tent. There was a full kitchen, a double bed, a stall shower, and the table in the dinette had been set up with all of her electronic equipment—fax, laptop, cellular phone, and a stereo with an attendant stack of compact discs.

"You sure you can make it, roughing it like this?"

"I'll manage," she said.

"I don't see any air-conditioning unit. You okay about breathing raw air?"

Paula knew she was being baited and refused to rise to it. "Central air," she answered lightly.

"And who's paying for this floating palace?"

"My department. This project has a very high priority."

"I'll bet it does," he said sourly. "How long do you

81

plan on being here?" He had the feeling her stay would not be brief.

"Three months," she said readily. "That's what the judge said."

"Don't you have a life?"

"It can wait." She bent to pick up a box of books. "Don't you have a life yourself?"

In spite of himself, Lovell jumped to help her with the heavy carton. "This is it." He pulled a book from the box. "*Autism and Ritual*," he read. "This is all about your career, isn't it?" He tossed the book back. "I was right. You're going to do make full professor on her back."

"You have a problem with that?" She fixed him with that challenging stare.

"Yes, as it happens. Nell isn't a laboratory rat. That cabin isn't a Skinner box."

Olsen stopped stowing her clothes and drew a deep breath in an attempt to keep control of herself. "You want to be helpful?" she asked sharply. "Why don't you stop acting like a jealous lover and cooperate? You want to be a Boy Scout, go ahead. But don't kid yourself that makes you of any more use to Nell. So I would appreciate it if you could do your best not to screw this up."

Lovell frowned and gritted his teeth. Olsen's piercing words struck a little too close to home. "Cooperate? That depends on what you're planning to do. Tell me what you plan to do and I'll tell you if I'm likely to screw it up."

"I plan to do as little as possible. I'm here to watch and listen and learn. No intervention, no contamination. We leave her alone until we find out the best way to help her. Observation and assessment, just like the judge said. Nothing more, nothing less." When the three months were up, Paula planned on presenting a report so compelling that Judge Hazan would have no option but to award guardianship of Nell to her and the psychiatric division of Seattle General Hospital.

"Kind of like bird watching?" said Lovell.

Olsen nodded and met his steady gaze. "Sure. Like bird watching . . ."

Lovell tried to steal into Nell's cabin like a cat burglar, moving as quietly as he could, inching his way across the porch and into the house one careful footfall after another. The door to the bedroom stood ajar slightly and he could see her stretched on the bed, asleep and curled around her slumbers.

Slowly, he slumped to the floor, afraid that the cracking of his joints would awaken her, and drew a small cassette recorder from his pocket. He poked the machine as far as he dared into the room, switched it on and waited. He sat very still, waiting in the gathering dusk.

After a while, Nell began to whimper, yet her eyes remained closed. A thin cry, a sound midway between a moan and a wail, came from the bedroom. *"Aiee . . . aiee . . ."*

The tenor of the sound was so plaintive, so mournful, that Lovell's heart went out to her.

Then, without warning, the cry stopped and another, more soothing voice took over. *"Doana kee, missa. Missa, chicka missa, doana kee . . ."*

The whimpering, melancholy voice returned. *"Nay tata, nay tata-kee. Nay, nay, be lilt, chickabee. Missa chickabee, lilten, lilten."*

The second voice was so gentle, so loving it sounded as if there were two different people in the bedroom. Listening to the two different sounds, Lovell's head swam with questions.

Then Nell's voice became more rhythmic became a chant, a soft strand of words in cadence. *"Lilten pogies, lilten dogies. Lilten sees, lilten awes. Lilten kine, lilten way. Lilten alo'lay . . ."*

Then silence.

Lovell carried his tape recording to Olsen and gave it to her, a peace offering.

"I think you'll find this interesting," he said. A peace offering it may have been, but he was unable to keep the slightest note of smugness from his voice, as if he had one-upped her, the country hick beating the slick professional at her own game.

Olsen listened to the tape and was—secretly—impressed, but her outward reaction was hardly what he expected. Delight, wonder, astonishment, rueful admission that she had been bested—he was prepared for any of those. Paula Olsen's spitting fury took him completely by surprise.

"What the hell do you think you're doing?" Paula yelled fiercely. "How dare you violate her private space?"

He was taken aback for a moment, but held his ground. "What's the matter? Jealous?"

Olsen shook her head in disgust. "Jesus, I thought we'd been through all this. Maybe you don't give a damn about what I'm trying to achieve around here, but how about some respect for Nell?"

"She's not a rare bird," he snapped. "She's a person. Listen—" He snapped on the cassette recorder. *"Nay, nay, be lilt, chickabee. Missa, chickabee, lilten, lilten . . ."* Nell's voice was tinny and thin in the cheap speaker, but the emotion of the words was unmistakable.

"I want to get to know her," said Lovell earnestly. "I want to learn her language."

It was a struggle, but Paula Olsen forced herself to calm down. Anger had had no effect on Lovell's stubbornness. Maybe it was time to try friendly persuasion.

"Okay . . . okay . . . Listen to me. This isn't a game."

"I know that."

"But do you have any idea how unusual this is? People just don't invent private languages. The analysis of language is a highly specialized field and you don't know anything about it."

"How do you know?"

Paula almost laughed. "Because *I* don't know anything about it."

Lovell waved away her faultless logic. "Doesn't matter anyway. I don't want to analyze her language. I want to talk to her."

"But why? *Why* do you want to talk to her?"

"Because I like her," said Lovell simply.

"You like her? Great. I like her. But we have to be professional about his."

Lovell nodded slowly, as if the truth had finally dawned on him. "Oh, I get it . . . we're professionals, so that means that we're not supposed to get involved with patients, right?"

Paula nodded. "That's right."

"Well, I say bullshit, Olsen. You are in Nell's life now and she's in yours. You're involved, whether you like it or not."

"You're impossible," she said, turning and walking back to the house boat. Her chest heaved and her cheeks were red as if the truth of his words had hit her smack in the face, like a slap.

ELEVEN

Dr. Amy Blanchard's long workday was just coming to an end. She was locking up the office and preparing to leave when Lovell piloted his Jeep into his customary parking place in front of his office. Dr. Blanchard did not look happy.

Lovell jumped out of the car, his hands up, as if she had a gun on him. "I'm sorry, I'm sorry. Don't even say it. I know how you feel."

"Really?" said Blanchard sourly. "How *do* I feel?"

"You want to kill me, right?"

Blanchard shook her head. "Wrong. You're no use to me dead, Jerry. Course you're not much use to me alive, not these days anyway."

Jerry Lovell winced. His partner looked and sounded worn out, drained with the effort of covering his patients as well as her own. "Wait till you hear this. I want three months leave of absence."

Amy seemed to sag, as if this was another burden on her shoulders. "Three months! Jerry, I can't—"

"I'll get a locum," he said quickly. "I won't draw a penny in fees. Anything you want, Amy. Just give me these three months. *Please*."

Amy Blanchard stared at him, as if trying to look in through his eyes and read his mind. "Why is she so important to you?"

"She needs me," Lovell said with a helpless shrug. "I can't leave her alone with those psychic vivisectionists."

"And what happens after three months?" asked Amy. "What then? Are you going to appoint yourself her guardian for life? This could go on for years."

"I don't know about years . . . Let's just see what happens in ninety days." He shuffled his feet in the dust. "I wouldn't ask if I didn't think it was important. I can give her a life, Amy."

"You're sure of that?"

"Yes I am." In fact, Lovell was plagued by self-doubt, unsure that he could do anything for Nell. But he was determined to keep her out of institutions, away from the prying and poking. Nell would never be a case study or an object of curiosity.

"Oh, Jerry . . ." she said with a sad shake of her head. "I guess if it's that important to you—" she shrugged and smiled ruefully. "What choice do I have?"

A wraith behind the glowing gauze of the curtain, Nell stood unmoving, staring into the night. She looked beyond the houseboat, as incongruous as a skyscraper would be in that place, to the trees and the lake, her eyes piercing into the night, as if watching something that no one else could see.

She began to hum, a low murmur, rising from her throat and filling the air. Nell felt herself melting away, fading into the sound and into her mind. Gradually Nell vanished, replaced by the twin girls, their faces grave and pale, the hum a wordless dialogue between them, a chain that bound them, as if they have found the place in which they became one person . . .

The red ball of the rising sun rose behind the silver disc of the lake, long garlands of light reflected in the water. There was a little splash, no more sound than a fish would make, and Paula Olsen broke the surface and slipped over on her back. She swam looking directly into the tranquil blue sky. Paula was a strong, sure swimmer and she barely made a ripple as she cut through the water, making for land.

The water was cold and invigorating, refreshing her tired body and mind. She had sat up late into the previous night reading and thinking, trying to unravel the enigma that was Nell.

She did not fit any of the profiles of wild children and her development seemed to have spiraled off on its own unique course. All of the feral children that had been studied had been confined, in most cases physically restrained, evinced some signs of mental retardation, and had been subjected to various forms of physical, psychological, and sexual abuse. A cursory examination of Nell suggested that she had not been abused and the blood test had ruled out any prenatal disease or debilitating childhood illness. Metabolic irregularities did not seem to enter into the equation either.

Olsen swam in long, easy strokes. These few minutes in the cold water would be her only relaxation that day. She was acutely aware that her time was limited, that three months would pass in a flash—and she knew from experience that a detailed case study could take years to conclude. Now she had to go from a standing start and break new ground on a unique case in a very short period. A difficult task at the best of times, but now she was buried in the wilderness, without access to a suitable laboratory or first-rate library, no senior colleagues for a professional opinion or judgment. And on top of all that, she did not have a free hand to act as she saw fit. She had Jerry Lovell.

As Paula's head bobbed above the water, she caught a glimpse of Lovell's Jeep driving into the clearing. She picked up the pace, kicking vigorously for the shore. She pulled herself from the water and shook her hair, then walked quickly toward the houseboat.

Lovell got out of his Jeep and was walking toward his tent when he stopped and looked at the cabin. Running across the middle of the clearing, strung in the lower branches of the trees, was a line of thick cable. It ran from Nell's cabin directly to the houseboat. Jerry followed the line with his eyes, then turned and strode toward the houseboat. Even from a distance, Olsen could tell he was angry.

By the time she got to her door, Lovell had let himself in and was staring, with horrified fascination, at a video monitor set on the table. The screen showed a wide view of a bedroom—Nell's bedroom—and Nell herself could be seen in the faint amber light, lying asleep on the bed. Judging by the angle of the shot, the camera seemed to have been mounted in the rafters, the place where Lovell first discovered her.

The low light softened the details of the scene, but the invasion could not have been more clear.

"You didn't say anything about video cameras to me," he said when Olsen entered. He was angry, but that didn't prevent him from noticing that Paula had been swimming in a T-shirt and very little else. The soaked cotton clung to her skin, delineating a very fine figure.

"It's a lot less intrusive than having you or me in there with her," she said. "If it makes you feel like a voyeur . . ." She gave a nonchalant shrug and she pulled a towel from a closet and wrapped it around herself. "That's something you'll have to work out for yourself."

"That's not the point," he snapped. "We had an agreement. You didn't check with me."

"All right," she said. "I'm checking now."

He stared at the image on the screen for a moment. Nell had scarcely moved under the covers and for the first time he saw her completely at peace, her guard down. He had to admit that Olsen had pulled off an amazing accomplishment, introducing the camera into Nell's home unobtrusively.

"You fixed this up in the night?"

Olsen nodded. "She never even woke up."

"How the hell did you manage that?"

"I was very quiet," she said, adding that knowing little smirk. "Didn't even need an electric drill. I used duct tape and G-clamps."

"The things you learn in graduate school," said Lovell, turning his attention to the screen.

Nell was waking up. Her eyes fluttered open and she sat up. Then she reached out with her left hand and lightly stroked the mirror next to the bed, caressing her own image.

"May I dress?" asked Olsen.

Lovell could not tear his eyes from the screen. "Yeah. Sure. In a minute."

"Now."

"Yeah, yeah," said Lovell, reluctantly heading for the door. He paused only to snatch the cassette tape she had made the day before. "Let me borrow this . . ."

Lovell spent the rest of the morning pacing the clearing, the earphones of a Walkman clamped to his head playing the tape of Nell's voice over and over again.

As he listened, he spoke along with the words, like an actor learning his lines. The most important part of the exercise—and also the most difficult—was matching the tone of Nell's voice, the key to the soft comfort of the words. The pitch of Nell's voice was much higher than his own, so he brought the timbre down to almost a whisper. As he repeated the words, their sense, if not their exact meaning, began to emerge.

"Nay, nay, be lilt, chickabee. Missa chickabee, lilten, lilten," he murmured. He had seen the effect on Nell of the word *"chickabee."* It had been immediate and profound, so strong that a single word had overwhelmed her deep-seated instincts of fear, flight, and self-preservation. Lovell imagined that chickabee must have been a term of endearment used by Violet Kellty, a word that Nell would have heard in the cradle, a word that meant love and security.

He snapped the tape into rewind and played the second half of the verse again. Nell's voice seemed to fill his head. *"Lilten pogies, lilten dogies . . . Lilten sees, lilten awes. Lilten kine, lilten way, lilten alo'lay . . ."*

"Lilt" and *"lilten"* were obviously calming words, sounds that lulled and soothed. The cadence was slow and tranquil, filled with a comforting peace. He couldn't guess at the meaning of the other words. But they would come in time.

TWELVE

As Jerry Lovell climbed the worn porch steps of the cabin, he heard a startled cry from Nell, followed by a mad scrabble, as she darted away into the interior of the house.

He was aware that every footfall brought terror to Nell and he hated scaring her, but he steeled himself and forced his way into the kitchen, then peered into the bedroom. Nell had retreated into her corner, hunched and tense, and she was watching him, her eyes filled with horror.

Very slowly Lovell sank to his knees, his hands open, palms out.

"There's nothing to be afraid of," he said, his voice low and calm. "Please don't be frightened." He inched toward her, not so near that he was threatening or risked crowding, but close enough that she could, for the first time, get a good look at him. But her face was blank and uncomprehending.

"My name is Jerry," he said. "Jerry." He raised a

finger and pointed at her. "Nell." Then he pointed to himself. "Jerry."

Nell's breath came fast and shallow, her chest heaving. Her eyes darted from side to side and she started to whimper, flailing her arms, her limbs jerking spasmodically. Lovell could tell that she was working toward a screaming fit and he had no choice but to play his trump card.

"Nay, nay," he said calmly. *"Be lilt chickabee."*

The effect of his words on Nell was dramatic. A look of astonishment crossed her features. Astounded, she blinked rapidly and then looked from side to side, as if the voice had come from somewhere else in the room. She would not look at him.

"Lilten, t'ee, lilten way. Lilten alo'lay."

Bit by bit, her nervous movements subsided into stillness and her breathing slowed. Her body seemed to uncoil slightly and she looked down to the floor. It was almost as if his words had cast a spell on her.

Lovell pressed on. *"Nay, nay be lilt, chickabee. Missa chickabee . . ."*

Nell raised her eyes to his. They were tear-filled and beseeching, loaded with a silent entreaty; she was begging him for something—something he could not fathom. He felt the constricting tightness of frustration—the two of them had managed to connect, but he could not go any further. He wanted to shout out loud and seize hold of her; he wanted to beg her to speak to him, to tell him what it was she wanted.

Lovell took a deep breath and tried to stay composed. Nell's demeanor would reflect his own. If he stayed calm she would also.

"Missa chickabee," he murmured.

He was wrong. Her calm vanished and she jumped, as if he had struck her with the full weight of his fist. She was panicked and he could see it. She crawled to the mirror, reached up to the glass, and attempted to stroke her face reflected there.

"Mi'i . . . mi'i . . ." she cried.

The tiny words came from her heart and Lovell ached for her. She began to rock rhythmically, her hands reaching out to her own image in the glass.

"Thee'n me an' me'n thee . . ." she whispered.

She pressed her whole hand against the mirror and leaned her forehead against the glass as if cooling her brow. In her mind, the glass gave way, as if it were the surface of a clear, still pool of water and for a moment the fingers of two hands intertwined. Nell and her twin knelt on the floor, hands clasped, brows touching.

"Mi'i," said Nell. She ran a finger down her face, caressing her own cheek. *"Mi'i . . ."*

"She has an objective self and a subjective self," said Olsen. "I've never seen such a perfect projection before."

"Indeed," said Professor Paley.

While Paula Olsen had been up in Richfield doing her fieldwork, Paley had been busy back in Seattle. He had brought in two other doctors, Harry Goppel, a behavioral scientist, and Jean Malinowski, an expert in childhood trauma. Goppel was a dyed-in-the-wool behaviorist, believing in the school of psychology that took objective evidence of behavior as the only basis of psychological makeup. To put it simply: Nell was the way she was because she was raised to be that way.

Jean Malinowski had seen too much of the dark side of life, had treated too many abused and mistreated children to be as sure as her colleague was about anything— particularly in the field of child development. Her job on the team was to observe Nell for any lingering signs of distress that may have occurred in her past and how it might affect her behavior in adulthood.

The four were gathered in the semidarkness of a

seminar room at Seattle General, listening to Olsen's report and watching a portion of the hours of videotape she had collected. "Nell's highlight reel," Lovell had called it.

On the tape, Nell was touching the mirror. *"Mi'i,"* she said. *"Mi'i."* Then she touched her cheek.

Olsen used a remote control to rewind the tape. "You see? Objective self." Nell touched the image in the mirror. Olsen speeded forward. "Subjective self."

"It's 'me' in the mirror," said Olsen.

"That's strange," said Goppel. "Don't you think?"

Olsen nodded. "Yes. You'd think it would be the other way round. But that's 'me' out there. It's almost as if she's displacing herself."

Nell's face was frozen on the screen. Goppel leaned forward to peer at her. "She seems to be crying."

"That's right," said Olsen. "Most likely a response to Dr. Lovell speaking to her in her own language. Tears would be a perfectly natural response."

"Her own language?" asked Goppel. "She has evolved her own language."

"It was a private language. She spoke it with her mother," said Olsen. "Her mother is recently deceased and suddenly a stranger appears speaking a language known only to her. Tears are entirely pertinent, in this instance."

Goppel shook his head, clearing it, as if not quite sure what he had heard. "Evolved her own language?"

Paley smiled. "Show Harry some Nellish, Paula . . ."

"Okay." Olsen consulted her notes and than ran the tape in reverse.

Jean Malinowski touched her own cheek, a clumsy imitation of Nell. "What was this gesture about?" she asked.

"Hard to say." Olsen frowned and looked at her notes. "It is an idiosyncratic gesture. It may be a form of pointing. Nell did it when she was indicating 'me.'" She stopped the tape and the screen went blank.

"Before we hear her speak, please try to remember that the speech degradation is misleading. The mother was dysphasic. But as to where the idiosyncratic word forms come from"—she shrugged and started the tape—"you tell me."

When the static cleared, they could see that Nell was sitting on her bed, her knees drawn up to her chest, her feet hooked over the edge of the mattress. Her arms encircled her slim legs, like the bands of a barrel holding together the staves. She was rocking gently and talking to herself in a low voice. Her voice was subdued, but her words were urgent, as if she was convincing herself of something.

"Ah si'fu' naish, ah peep'u lai'wi neek'ty," she murmured. *"Ah see o'eva'dur . . ."*

Goppel and Malinowski watched her, transfixed by her actions and the sounds of her voice. Even Paley and Olsen, both of whom had seen the tape before, seemed fascinated.

Finally Goppel spoke. "It's incredible."

Nell's voice became more intense. *"Ah ha' fo'sa a'law, ah ha' pro' fo' a ho'y un a'Isa'el . . ."*

The picture on the screen was grainy and jumpy, the sound had the hollow tone produced by an open mike, filtered through a tinny speaker, but Nell and her speech were completely arresting. The four experts strained to hear every syllable and watched every movement.

"Are there transcripts of her talk?" asked Goppel.

"I've done my best, but it's not easy to render exactly," said Olsen. "As you can hear, the recordings are a little on the primitive side."

"If the need arises, we can get a trained philologist to work up a more precise transcript." Paley looked to his own notes. "The most important thing now is to compile a case for the transfer of care. Once the legal matters are settled our job will be that much easier."

The professor spoke as if the judicial questions were nothing more than minor inconveniences. Paula Olsen looked more skeptical and wished she could share her mentor's confidence.

"There is no possibility of transferring her here?" asked Malinowski. She smiled diffidently at Olsen. "Paula, your work so far has been marvelous, but substantive study can't be done in the field."

Goppel agreed. "This isn't medical care, as much as it's anthropology."

Paula Olsen did her best to hide her scowl and to keep her anger out of her voice. But she didn't back down either, taking Goppel head on. "The court has ruled that she cannot be taken from her home. It's as simple as that. We will mount a challenge to the ruling when the three months are up; in the meantime we'll have to work with what we have." Olsen looked from Malinowski to Goppel. "*I* have no problems with living up there. You could say that studying Nell on her home turf is *exactly* the place for substantive study."

"I don't agree," said Malinowski quickly.

"That's your prerogative, Doctor," said Olsen.

Paley moved quickly to quell the discord. "The court and Lovell are problems that will be dealt with in due course. For the time being—Paula, keep up the good work." He smiled warmly, but his words seemed to suggest that she would do well to remember that she was the junior member of the team.

"Lovell?" said Goppel. "Who's Lovell?"

Paula rolled her eyes. "Jerry Lovell is the local doctor who has appointed himself the protector of Nell. He was the one who filed the lawsuit."

"A country doctor? What is he? A GP?" He smiled thinly. Olsen got the distinct feeling that Dr. Goppel did not have much respect for general practitioners. Special-ization was the way to the top of the medical profession.

"You want to know an interesting fact?" said Paley. "Lovell is not, as it happens, a mere country doctor."

"He isn't?" said Olsen. Somehow this information did not surprise her as much as it ought.

"Nope. Three years ago, Jerome Lovell was a senior consultant in pediatric oncology at Children's Hospital."

"You've been checking up on him?"

"I like to know who's questioning my professional decisions," said Paley. "I have to admit, I was surprised at the depth of his credentials."

"Which are?" asked Goppel.

"Physicians and Surgeons in New York," said Paley, sounding genuinely impressed. "That was followed by a stint at the Farber Institute in Boston . . . Not bad for a country GP."

"Pediatric oncology," said Olsen. "That explains a lot as regards Nell."

"How do you mean?" asked Malinowski.

"I asked him if he always gets this involved with his patients. He said: 'I try.' " Olsen suddenly looked sad. "I can't think of a more *involving* practice than children and cancer."

"Well," said Paley, "he's not involved anymore." He closed his file and stood up. It was apparent that he was bringing the meeting to a close.

"What happened?" asked Olsen. "He walked out?"

Paley shrugged. "Did he walk or was he pushed? We have a court hearing coming up in a few weeks. Let's not have him get in the way again."

To Paula's surprise, Al Paley insisted on walking Paula to her car.

"Just between us, Paula, what are we going to do about Dr. Lovell?"

Paula shrugged and grimaced. "What can I do? I told

him not to go into the cabin. I told him to leave her alone. But he cares, right? So in he goes."

"You're doing a good job. Just be sure this doesn't go sour on us. It's too important."

"What am I supposed to do? Drag him out by the hair?"

Paley stopped and faced Paula square on. "Dr. Lovell thinks he's Nell's only friend, right? Her champion against the forces of darkness?"

"Yes. Something like that."

Paley started walking again. "Then handle him with care, Paula. People like him—they're the ones who sue. Hell haith no fury like a member of the caring professions scorned."

"So what are you saying? Back off? Let him trample all over Nell?"

"I'm not saying that . . . just find a way to work with him, get him on your side. It's only ten weeks till we go to court. You can be extremely charming when you want to be."

Paula burst into laughter. "You want me to seduce the guy? *Puh*-leeze!"

Unaware that his past—and his future—were being discussed in a seminar room many miles away, Jerry Lovell was seated on the floor of Nell's bedroom, exhilarated at the progress he was making with her. She accepted his presence now, but was still wary enough to keep her distance, not daring to get closer to him. She circled the room, reaching out to stroke the mirror everytime she passed it. She never looked directly at Lovell, but watched from the corner of her eye, aware of his every movement.

"Nell?" he said.

There was no response. He tried the words that got a

reaction the last time. *"Missa chickabee,"* he said. Nell did not speak, but she paused in her circuit of the room, as if to show that his words had an affect on her. After a moment, she started again.

"You mind if I talk?"

He took her silence to imply consent.

"Okay . . ." He looked around the room, taking in the patterns of light and shadow in the cabin. "I like it here," he said. "It's a quiet place."

Nell circled the room, Lovell remained slouched in the corner. His voice was low, his words slow, as if feeling his way, more or less talking to himself.

"You know what? You've got the right idea. You live with people, you get problems. First they screw you up, then they leave you, right?

"Do you ever get lonely, Nell?" He was tired and the Irish underpinnings of his accent seemed more pronounced this night.

Nell was silent.

"I never had any brothers or sisters," he said, as if she could understand every word. "That's very unusual for an Irish family. Oh sure, you better believe it . . . There was a family lived next door, the Connors, they have seven kids. Seven!" He grinned at Nell, as if daring her to believe that a family could be so large. "Always yelling and screaming. Having a good time. Me watching . . ." He framed his hands around his face. "Me watching through the window."

He retreated further into his memory, letting his past run like a piece of old, grainy film. "I remember once I was at home when I heard music. Brass band . . . There was this parade, you see, coming down the street. Kids running in front. The band was really loud, you know. I ran out on to our front steps—but that's as far as I went . . . Till Jamie Connor comes running over from next door and grabs my hand, pulls me into the street."

Slowly, he stood, becoming animated as he relived the memory. Nell was staring at him now. "The band was playing. Jamie's got my hand, we're doing this—" He swung his arms up high. "—ta-ra-ra-boom-di-ay! I'm swinging down the street. Some kids got my other hand—" He swung his other arm, high up. Both arms were going now, swinging in an exaggerated march. "Ta-ra-ra-ra! Ta-roo-roo-ray! Right behind me. The trumpets and the trombones and the big bass drum . . . You get close to a brass band, you know about it. I'm marching, I'm with the other kids—Boom-ba-ba, boom-ba-ba—Do you know what I'm saying? I wasn't alone. We weren't talking—just—"

His arms swaying, his body swaying, his face was alive with the joy of that summer day so many years ago. Nell had stopped circling. She was standing still, staring at him.

"Ga'inja," she said softly.

Without a trace of fear or hesitation she walked toward him. Lovell froze, his arms still high, not daring to move a muscle for fear of breaking this moment of concentration.

"Ga'inja come leess'a Nell," she said, gazing at him. *"J'ey ga'inja?"*

He could tell it was a question but all he could do was attempt to mimic her words. *"J'ey ga'inja,"* he said.

Her response was as immediate as it was unexpected. Suddenly a great, golden, dazzling smile burst from her, a smile that lit up her pale face. Nell's eyes sparkled with happiness and for a moment Jerry found himself caught in her sudden beauty.

But there was more. It was as if a barrier had been broken, as if a basic trust had been established and it brought forth a flood of words and gestures.

Nell intertwined her fingers and locked them together. *"Fo'tye maw done waw wi'a law, she—"* Her voice changed abruptly, as if imitating another voice. *"Nell, Nell done kee, kee, onakowna maw bin fearly, maw done go leess'a."*

Her eyes swept across his face, looking to him to see if he comprehended. It seemed that she was inviting him into her world, telling him something of profound importance to her and to the way she lived.

"Nell—" he said, unsure of how to proceed. The one thing he could see was that Nell was speaking, communicating. This flood of words proved that she did speak a language, a language as complex and as alive as any other.

As if to underscore this, Nell spoke again, as if she wanted to clarify or amplify what she had said already. She stroked her cheek lightly, that soft, characteristic caress that seemed to be as much a part of her vocabulary as any of her passionate words.

"Yo'kay? Maw done say af'ah done go, enja come, anna Nell bin feliss, anna lilten, anna erna feliss. Reckon?" Again she looked at him questioningly and again she was requesting a response.

He couldn't help but be buoyed by her sudden enthusiasm and display of trust.

"Reckon," he said, emphatically.

"Je'y enja?"

Lovell nodded vigorously. *"Jerry ga'inja."*

On her hands and knees, Nell began to crawl toward him. Her movements were uncertain and tentative but when she stopped she raised her right hand, palm out, facing him. It was the same gesture he had seen her make in the mirror. Lovell raised his left hand and placed it against hers. They were still for a moment—Lovell scarcely daring to breathe—then their fingers intertwined, two hands braided together as if in prayer.

"Je'y kine'ey ga'inja, reckon?" Nell whispered.

Lovell nodded, feeling the meaning of her words. *"Jerry kine'ey ga'inja."*

THIRTEEN

Beneath the emotion and elation of his breakthrough morning with Nell, Lovell was surprised to find that there was another, more subtle sensation—the desire to tell Paula Olsen all that had transpired.

He waited for her to return, his impatience growing as the hours ticked away. Invading the houseboat, Lovell found the tape of his encounter and played it time and again until he had memorized every word, every accent and gesture. The tape was so absorbing that he forgot his impatience and the passage of time and did not hear Olsen drive her car into the clearing.

"Make yourself at home," she said. Lovell jumped and turned. Olsen was framed in the doorway, smiling at him, bemused to find him so consumed with the images on the screen.

"You won't believe what happened," he said. The excitement in his voice was apparent, but then he turned suspicious. "Where have you been?"

"Miss me?" she asked. Olsen did not want to reveal

that she had been conferring with the people that Jerry Lovell would no doubt consider the enemy. She found that her attitude toward Lovell had undergone something of a change. The condescending and disdainful attitude of Doctors Paley, Goppel, and Malinowski toward Lovell had annoyed her, not to mention her irritation at their patronizing airs toward Olsen herself. Furthermore, the revelation of Lovell's past had intrigued her.

Lovell shook his head. "You missed the breakthrough, a great leap forward."

"Show me."

Lovell cued up the tape and then retreated to the rear of the houseboat, silently watching Olsen watch the tape. She ran it through twice before commenting, then turned to face him.

"Astonishing," she said simply.

"She talked. To me."

Olsen nodded. "That's right."

"Hold out your hand."

Paula knew what he meant and she put out one hand, palm forward, as Nell did. Lovell's palm met hers and their fingers intertwined. "I didn't ask for that," Lovell said. "She did."

Paula pulled her hand away. She was experiencing the faintest stab of jealousy. "Yeah, I know."

"Je'y ga'inja."

"You know what it means?"

"No."

Paula Olsen rewound the tape and together they went through it, second by second, frame by frame. She was compiling a word list, noting down every expression with her guess at the possible meanings.

"It's English," she said. "I'm pretty sure of that now. Some of it is pretty straightforward, even accounting for the speech distortion. *Tye* is time. *Spee*—speak. She's

106

dropping the last consonants." She ran a part of the tape at normal speed. Nell's voice filled the room.

"Af'I done go, enja come," she said. Olsen hit the pause button, freezing Nell on the screen. "See? There's only one word of pure Nellish there." She ran the tape again.

"Nellish?" Lovell shook his head and smiled. "Fantastic, isn't it?"

"She wanted you to be *'ga'inja'*" said Olsen. "When you agreed to be *ga'inja*—that's when she put out her hand."

"Jerry enja," said Lovell. *"Jerry kine'ey ga'inja."*

"Friend? Do you think that could be it?"

Lovell shrugged. "Could be . . . whatever it is, it's an important concept to her. It was the key to making further contact."

"Of course, we're really no closer to answering the bigger question."

"Which is?"

"Where are these words coming from? Language grows and evolves from outside influences. Do you have any idea how unusual it is, a private language?"

"Some. Never really thought about it."

Olsen stared at the image on the screen, watching the moment of hand contact. Olsen spoke without taking her eyes off the arresting image.

"She trusts you." She watched, observing Lovell more this time than Nell, surprised at the small, gentle gestures from the big man, his sensitive, reassuring tone of voice. "You're good with her."

Lovell was surprised. A compliment from this cool, critical woman—that was a first. "How about that? I actually did something right."

"Right," said Olsen with a small smile. "And you deserve a reward. How about a beer?"

"You read my mind."

They settled in two folding beach chairs under the canvas awning next to Lovell's tent. The air was still warm and the breeze was light, but the rays of the setting sun were long orange beams across the water. The only sound was the soft chirr of insects in the underbrush.

He looked out over the lake. "You've got to admit, this is not a bad place to live."

"Tell Nell. Maybe she'll come out and take a dip in the lake." She proffered one of the cold cans. "Beer?"

Lovell took it, popped it, and took a long pull. "She does. At night. She swims in the lake."

Olsen looked taken aback. "She does? How do you know that?"

"I've seen her."

"You never told me." The old wariness was beginning to creep over her again. Olsen had forgotten, for the moment, that they were in competition.

"I'm telling you now."

"So what did you see?" She glanced at her houseboat, wondering if she should go and get her notebook.

"She came out of her cabin, went to the end of the jetty, stripped naked, and plopped herself in the water." He took another swig of beer and found that he derived a great satisfaction from surprising his rival.

"That's it?"

Lovell nodded. "That's it."

"Did she look like she was afraid?" Olsen asked. Swimming was a conditioned response in humans. In other words, it did not come naturally but had to be taught and learned.

"Afraid? No, she wasn't afraid." He thought of Nell's trusting backward fall into the black water, the heart-stopping length of time she spent submerged, followed by that sudden, joyous burst from the deep. "Far from it."

"And she didn't mind being naked?" Olsen asked.

Lovell shook his head. "Nope. Not in the least."

"How about you?" she asked with a sly smile. "Did *you* mind?"

"I thought she was beautiful." Lovell didn't smile, his expression was disapproving, almost prim. It was plainly not a subject open to a little good-natured banter.

Paula sipped her own beer and considered his reaction. A few days before she had accused him of acting like a jealous lover toward Nell. Now she wondered if maybe she hadn't struck a nerve.

"She's beautiful," Paula said matter-of-factly. "Is that why you're so interested in her?"

This time Lovell did smile. "You are asking me if I'm planning to abuse the doctor-patient relationship. Is that what's on your mind?"

Olsen nodded. "Are you?"

"No," said Lovell. "Just because she's beautiful doesn't mean I want to have sex with her. I think you're beautiful, but—" He shrugged, a gesture that said "naturally, I'm not interested."

"Gee, thanks," said Olsen with a hollow laugh.

"You know what I mean." Lovell squirmed slightly, as if suddenly aware that he had embarrassed Olsen as well as himself.

"Yeah, yeah," she said with an offhand wave. "That's okay." She was not offended—more amused, if anything. She settled deeper in her chair and sipped her beer. She was unwinding, relishing the warm rays of the waning sun, the peace, and the quiet. She had no stomach for a fight, not right at that moment, anyway—when the time for battle came, she would be ready.

"You know something," said Olsen. "When I was thirteen, my father said to me, 'You're so beautiful, you're almost perfect.'" She smiled ruefully. "Almost. That 'almost' really got under my skin. 'So what's wrong with me,' I said. 'Nobody's perfect,' he said to me."

Lovell nodded. "Dad's right,"

"Sure, but this was *me* we were talking about," she said, laughing. "I kept on at him. What is it? What's wrong with me? Why aren't I perfect? Is it my thighs? No. My teeth? No. My tits? No."

"You said 'tits' to your father?"

"Well . . . Not in so many words . . ." She took another sip of her beer. "I went on and on at the poor man until finally he told me."

"I know from experience how much fun you are to be around when you've got a bee in your bonnet."

"Care to guess what my father thought was an imperfection?"

Lovell shrugged. "No idea."

"It's my ears, he tells me. They stick out."

"They do?" said Lovell. "Move your hair. Let me see."

Paula shook her head vigorously and put her hands over her ears like headphones. "Nope."

"C'mon."

"Absolutely not," she said emphatically. "They stick out. Not much. Hardly at all, not so as anybody would ever notice. But it bugged me—my ears aren't perfect. And you know what? I've never been able to show my ears since."

Lovell grinned. "You could always have them fixed you know. A good plastic surgeon could do it in twenty minutes."

"You think I should?" He was kidding, of course, but Olsen appeared to take his suggestion seriously.

"What do I know?" he said. "I've never seen them— but no, I don't think you should have them fixed. No unnecessary surgery. That's one of my rules for living."

"No drugs, no surgery. You're some doctor."

"It's simple," said Lovell. "The focus of anxiety changes, the level of anxiety remains the same. Lovell's law."

"Which states?"

110

"If your fix your ears, you start worrying about your weight. Get your weight down and the next thing you know you're worrying about cancer. See?"

"Thanks," said Olsen. "That's some progression. I start out with sticking-out ears, I end up with cancer."

"You know what I'm saying," Lovell insisted. "It makes sense, doesn't it?"

She was quiet for a moment, trying to decide if she should press on, to pry—she was nothing if not relentlessly curious.

"Funny you should mention cancer," she said finally.

"Funny? I don't know how funny it is."

"I heard you were a cancer specialist."

Lovell's smile was shrewd and knowing. "You heard?" He nodded slowly. "Know your enemy, huh?" It was obvious that Olsen had been checking up on him.

"Something like that," she admitted.

"Anyway . . . I *was* a cancer specialist."

"What happened there?"

"Simple," said Lovell. "I quit."

"Why?"

Lovell fidgeted and twisted, as if physically trying to dodge the questions. "I had my reasons . . . personal reasons. Let's just leave it at that."

"I told you about my ears," Olsen protested. "It's the least you could do."

"But there's nothing wrong with your ears."

"How do you know? You haven't seen them."

Lovell leaned forward and smiled. "Okay. Go on. Show them to me."

"No."

"There you go. A standoff."

Olsen and Lovell grinned and sipped their beers. They both felt the same thing—that they had reached a small turning point, perhaps the birth of a friendship. From now on they would be studying each other, as well as Nell.

FOURTEEN

The sunlight through the trees cast a delicate lattice of shadows on the fabric-covered window of Nell's bedroom. She stood by the window, carefully tracing the lacy fretwork of silhouettes that tremored slightly in the breeze. Her fingers were long, slim, and delicate, the skin surprisingly soft for one who had been raised in the rough.

Although Nell seemed to be intent on the simple task at hand, outlining the pale gray shapes on the old muslin, Lovell could see that she was deep in thought. It was as if an internal debate was taking place in her mind, as she pondered whether or not to go forward to the next step in their tentative friendship.

She seemed to make up her mind, deciding in favor, but slowly and reluctantly, cautiously.

"Missa kine," Nell said. She did not look up from the shadows and her eyes remained fixed on her fingers as they worked their way around the shadows. *"Missa kine. Yo'kay?"*

"I don't understand," said Lovell.

Now she turned to him. *"Shie done come, durda come feliss a'missa kine."* Her words were earnest and heartfelt. She pointed to one of the shadows. *"Missa kine."*

"Missa?" asked Lovell. "What is *missa*, Nell?"

Nell nodded and crouched down, making herself as small as possible, using her body in demonstration much the way a child might.

"Missa Nell," she said. Then she stood up, throwing her shoulders back, squaring them, making herself as tall as possible. *"Erna Nell."*

Lovell nodded. He put his hands close together. *"Missa?"*

Nell nodded.

He widened the space between his hands. *"Erna?*

"Big and small," said Lovell.

Nell nodded again. *"Yo'kay."*

"What is *kine*, Nell? *Kine?"*

Nell nodded and closed her eyes and raised her arms, spreading them wide. She swayed slightly, bending at the waist, her head lolling loosely from side to side. As she mimed, she made a soft hissing sound.

Lovell studied her for a moment or two, enchanted by the grace and fluidity of her lithe movements. "You're a tree," he said. "A tree in the wind."

Nell nodded. *"Kine inna way."*

"Tree in the wind," said Lovell slowly, carefully enunciating every word.

"T'ee inna win'?"

"Yes. That's right." Cautiously, as if some sudden movement would startle her, Lovell moved toward the door and opened it a few inches.

"Show me, Nell. Show me *'kine.'"*

Nell's mood changed immediately. Her eyes went wide, then narrowed, her face darkened with fear. She shrunk away from the open door as if there were something intensely evil on the other side of it.

"*Nay, Nell tata,*" she said, shaking her head. "*Nell erna* tata. *Erna tata.*"

"*Tata?*" asked Lovell. "What's *tata*?"

Nell didn't have to act it out this time. She was hunched over, almost trembling with fear. The word meant terror, pure and simple.

"Why *tata*, Nell?" asked Lovell. "What is making you so afraid?"

Nell's eyes flashed and her words tumbled from her in a torrent. "*Inna tye'a shie, eva'dur done come, eva'dur done yow Nell, done— Yaah! Hai! Hai! Zzzzzslit!*"

"Nell, *eva'dur*? Show me *eva'dur.*"

Nell bared her teeth, her hands formed into claws, raking the air. Her nostrils were flared and a snarling growl erupted from her throat.

Lovell narrowed his eyes and studied her closely. "A monster, Nell? Is *eva'dur* a monster?"

Nervously her eyes darted to the open door, as if eva'dur could come bursting in at any moment. Lovell closed it firmly and she seemed to relax a little, but she was still wary and on her guard. She looked back to the muslin curtain, but the shadows had vanished. The sun was setting and the night was closing in around them.

"Don't be afraid," said Lovell. "There's nothing to be afraid of. Really."

There was another cascade of talk from Nell. "*Eva'-dur done go inna tye'a feliss, Nell done caw Mi'i, done go alo'lay,*" she said vigorously. "*Nell leess'a Mi'i, leess'a Mi'i, aw tye. Missa chickabee. Yo'kay.*"

Lovell was lost in this web of words, recognizing few of them. He had no idea what she was saying, but it seemed so important to her that he grasp what she was saying he was forced to smile and nod. "*Yo'kay*, Nell, *yo'kay.*"

Nell nodded, relaxed and happy, but she turned away from him, retreating to her corner, as if signaling that the interview was at an end.

Lovell burst from the cabin, excited, elated, confused—his mind reeling at what had transpired. He was beginning to realize that Nell's world was a more complex place than he had thought. It was a living place, populated with creatures that existed in her imagination but which were real nonetheless. She had not been raised in, nor did she live in, a vacuum—she was not a child, her mind was not tabula rasa, but complex and complicated.

Olsen emerged from the houseboat, her notebook in her hand. "I saw it," she said. "I watched the whole thing on the monitor. I've added those words to the list."

"She is amazing," said Lovell, taking the notebook. "*Missa*—little," he read. "*Erna*—big. *Tata*—frightened. *Kine*—tree."

"So what's *eva'dur*?" asked Olsen. "Whatever it is, it certainly gets her worked up."

"It's something extremely aggressive," said Lovell. "Something that scares the hell out of her."

Olsen nodded. "And it isn't around at night. That's strange. In the mind the night is full of dangers. Yet Nell is not afraid to come out at night."

"Yeah," said Lovell. "What kind of monsters aren't around at night?"

"Imaginary ones."

"Well, that's obvious, but Nell believes they're real. Even if you don't speak her language you can hear the certainty in her voice."

"They don't come from Nell's imagination," said Olsen. "Remember, her sole source of information was her mother. I'd bet that Violet Kellty invented the monsters—the *eva'dur*—and put them in the day rather than the night. Told her daughter scare stories to keep her shut away. She kept her hidden for almost thirty years. The chance of someone seeing her at night, out here— just about zero, I'd say."

Lovell was studying the transcript. "*Eva'dur done go inna tye'a feliss*. In the . . . *tye* . . . That's time, I guess. The time of *feliss* . . . Darkness? Night? Something like that?"

"Probably," said Olsen.

On the far side of the clearing something moved, a small, darting motion that Lovell caught in the corner of his eye. It was the merest slip of white whispering away between the tall pines. It was Nell.

"She's out!" called Lovell.

Paula Olsen looked around quickly. "Where?"

Nell's slight figure glided into the night, stealing out of sight even as Lovell set off in pursuit. He plunged into the forest, crashing through the underbrush, his footsteps muffled by the thick carpet of pine needles on the ground. In among the trees the shadows were deep and it was impossible to see where Nell had gone. There was no path and she moved silently, scarcely disturbing the tangled undergrowth that was blocking Lovell's way.

He stopped in a thicket of thorn and gorse, listening, straining to hear Nell. The only sound was his own breathing. The air under the trees was cooler than the air in the clearing and it smelled damp and loamy.

Paula Olsen came crashing through the brush startling Lovell for a moment.

"Where is she?" Olsen asked.

"I don't know."

"Should we look for her?"

"Where?" Lovell shook his head. "She knows where she's going. We don't."

"Where do you think she's going?"

"Who can say?" He was still for a second or two

117

longer, as if hoping that Nell would reveal her where-abouts. But she was gone. And they were deep in the forest. "We better get back while there's still some light."

Olsen and Lovell had run farther into the forest than they thought and it was a long, bothersome walk back through the brambles to the clearing. They were both hot and sweaty by the time they made it back to the houseboat and Olsen disappeared inside. She reemerged a moment later with a chilled bottle of wine and a corkscrew, handing them to Lovell.

"She's certainly adapted to her environment," said Paula. "We could hardly move in there, but she went through that forest like she was on a highway."

"She's certainly full of surprises. Course, I would have put it another way. I would have said that she knows her way around. But there again, *I'm* not an academic." Lovell extracted the cork with a satisfying pop. "Glasses?"

For once, Paula Olsen did not bother to rise to his baiting. "Glasses, right."

Lovell listened to her banging around inside the kitchen as she opened and closed the cupboard doors, taking stock of her supplies. "I hope you feel like eating pasta. That's about all I have in stock."

"Sounds great."

Paula returned with the glasses. Lovell poured and they raised their cups as if in toast.

"Are we drinking to anything in particular?" she asked.

He shrugged. "Nell?"

"Why did I have the feeling you would say that?"

"You're adapting to your environment."

It did not take long for Paula Olsen to make a bowl of very satisfying pasta, a simple, aromatic concoction of tomatoes, garlic, and basil. They ate outside, under the canvas awning, a battery-powered lantern throwing a soft light over the table. Most of the wine had been consumed, in large part by Lovell, and the mood between them was relaxed and calm, although from time to time Olsen stared into the darkness of the forest.

"Where does she go?" she wondered. "I mean, what is there out in the woods?"

Lovell had to swallow the forkful of spaghetti in his mouth before he could reply. "You said it before. It's her forest."

"She *could* still get lost, she's not a mountain man. I don't want to lose her. I'm worried about her. It's dark out there."

"She likes the night."

Paula refused to be consoled. "She could fall down a ravine or something."

"You sound just like my mother."

"I am *not* your mother," she said sternly.

"Play in the yard, Jerry." He raised his voice an octave and spoke in an exaggerated Irish brogue. "Stay where I can see you, Jerry. Be careful, Jerry, you could get hurt."

Olsen laughed. "How Irish are you?"

"My mother's Irish. Dad's Boston born and bred. We lived in Ireland till I was sixteen. My father wanted me to have an Irish soul and an American income."

"Like him?"

Lovell grinned. "Bingo. He wanted me to be like him. *Boy*, did he want me to be like him!"

"And you weren't?"

"What do you think?"

"Sorry . . ." Paula's eyes scanned the darkness. "I wish she'd come back. I am worried that something will happen to her."

"Can't have that, right?" said Lovell. "You've got a theory to prove." A small smile took some of the sting out of his reproach.

"Fuck you too, Lovell." But there was no real hostility behind her comeback. She sipped her wine. "You think I'm only interested in Nell for myself, don't you?"

He put down his fork and stared at her for a moment, weighing his words carefully. "I think you're interested in Nell as a phenomenon," he said. "I think you see her as a problem, and you want to find the solution." He raised his eyebrows questioningly. "Right?"

Olsen was surprised. Maybe it was the mellowing influence of the wine, maybe it was just that he was tired of fighting with her, but he was close to being right on the mark.

"That's part of it," she said. "I happen also to think I can really make a difference to her life. Don't you?"

He refilled his glass and when she refused more, he took her measure for himself. "I'm not sure," he said quietly. "I'm really not sure."

"You *have* to be sure," Olsen said ardently. "You have to believe you have something to give her, or what are you doing here?"

"Don't you ever find yourself getting into something and you don't really know why?"

"Nope," she said emphatically.

Lovell turned back to his food and worked his fork in the tangle of pasta. "You think you're in control of your life?"

"I'd better be."

He shook his head slowly, as if amazed with the audacity of youth. "Then you're lucky. Pure, dumb luck—not control. It's as simple as that. You haven't messed up yet."

"And you have?"

He was silent for a long time, as if trying to decide whether or not she could be trusted with a secret. "Just that once," he said finally. He sighed heavily, as if relieved to have taken her into his confidence.

"Is that why you quit your job?"

"Yes."

"Someone died."

Lovell winced. She had found a bruise and she had pushed it hard. "Yeah."

The tireless investigator in Paula Olsen was beginning to assert itself. For a moment Jerry Lovell had ceased to be simply the man she was having dinner with and had become a case history, a knot of problems to be unraveled. She considered what she knew about Lovell and applied it to the mystery at hand.

"Misdiagnosis?" she asked.

"Mistreatment," he said grimly. "With cancer patients, the drug dosage is critical." He took a large gulp of wine as if it would anesthetize him to the torment of the memory.

"It happens." Her prosecutorial air began to slip away. The pain on his face was obvious and it touched her too.

"That's what they all said. One of those things. Nobody's fault. Sure." He shrugged and tried to smile. "But . . . it happened. It happened to me. And I guess, more important, . . . it happened to her."

"Her? Who was it?"

"A fourteen-year-old girl." He looked to Olsen for a moment, then his eyes darted away. "Annie."

The word, the name, seemed to hang in the air between them. Paula was silent, asking no more questions. If Lovell wanted to say more, he would; if not, she had no business trying to drag his past out of him.

Lovell was staring into the darkness, as if the cheerless events of the past were being acted out in front of him. He could see Annie, her bright eyes and her tangle of dark curls. A smile that was always hopeful even through her pain and fear. "I never told her I could cure her," he said. His voice was heavy, his eyes sad. "But she knew

121

I'd do anything that could be done . . . And what I did was kill her."

"Would she have died anyway?" Olsen asked.

"Of course," he said sharply. "We're all going to eventually . . ." Then his anger softened.

"Probably. The cancer was very advanced. She would have lived a little longer if I hadn't screwed up . . ." He took a small sip of wine and then smiled wearily. "I used to play her music. Old sixties tracks. Her parents thanked me afterward. Said I'd meant a lot to Annie, made the last weeks bearable."

He was silent for a very long time. Minutes passed. He didn't move, he didn't look at her. Lovell just sat, his eyes locked on the bulb of the lantern, his plastic beaker of wine growing warm between his hands.

Paula Olsen was beginning to think that he would say no more that night when he took up the story again. "Her parents . . . She loved those songs, they said."

"It never got out?" Olsen asked. "The parents never knew that the drug dose was incorrect?"

Lovell smiled crookedly and shook his head. "No. Of course not. Hospitals don't make those kind of mistakes. Too expensive, right? The club takes care of its own, you know. All the other physicians rallied round and kept it quiet." He drained his wine and exhaled heavily. "Can't risk pushing those malpractice insurance rates even higher, right . . ."

More than anything, Paula wanted to ease his pain. "If every doctor who screwed up went and quit there wouldn't be any doctors left."

"Yeah. They didn't want me to go."

"But you went."

Lovell nodded. "But that was the end for me. I knew it was over, even if they didn't."

Perhaps Lovell had convinced himself that his resignation was something he did for himself, but Paula thought she knew better. As a psychologist, she was well aware that there was no more punishing, excoriating human emotion than guilt. It was a relentless, day-in, day-out demon that burned through the soul like acid. Lovell was consumed by remorse over the death of a fourteen-year-old girl and, what's more, he wanted—demanded—punishment. He had buried himself up here in the mountains, a time-honored rite of penitence and expiation, making himself a troglodyte to repent of his great sin.

There was little she could say to make him feel better. The time-honored nostrums—*it could have happened to anyone, it was nobody's fault, it happens every day*—would sound shallow and flat, fatuous clichés that would probably only serve to make him feel worse.

Then there was a splash in the water. Lovell and Olsen looked to the left and saw Nell, her slim white body cutting through the dark water. She was no more than twenty yards from where they sat, the houseboat and the canvas awning awash in light—there was no way she could not know they were there—yet Nell showed not the slightest trace of shyness. She was completely absorbed in the delight of her play, cavorting in the swelling water like a sprite.

Paula and Jerry stared. Both of them felt as if they were seeing a different Nell, a free and happy woman emerging from the water as if cleansed of her fear and confusion. As she leapt in the water, Olsen took her eyes off her long enough to look at Lovell. He was watching her in rapt attention, his recent pain clearing from his face.

"You're right," Paula whispered. "She is beautiful."

Lovell did not take his eyes off Nell. He couldn't help but smile at her, the sheer joy of her enjoyment radiating.

"Why don't you play her some music?" Paula said. Lovell turned to meet Olsen's questioning glance. They both knew what she was saying—through the music, let the memory of Annie be healed through Nell.

Lovell hesitated only a moment before rising and entering the houseboat. Nell swam back to the jetty and without a shred of self-consciousness pulled herself out of the water in a single lithe movement. Water streamed from her limber arms and legs and she gave herself a shake, the way a dog does after being in the water, and reached for her jersey.

She was dressed and hurrying across the clearing toward the cabin when Lovell came out of the houseboat. Nell's manner had changed, her shoulders were hunched slightly and her eyes were downcast, as if she was less comfortable on land, as if the lake was her true home.

Suddenly the calm of the night was broken by a sequence of piano notes, sharp and clear in the still night air. Then the deep and evocative voice singing lazily.

"Crazy . . ." Patsy Cline's voice began the familiar and plaintive song. The lyrics seemed to curl and weave, meandering through the clearing like a coil of wood smoke.

The effect of the resonant music was sudden and abrupt. Nell came to an immediate and complete standstill, as if she had been pinned to a spot on the path by an invisible arrow. It was plain that she had never heard anything like it in all her life and the sound seemed to pass straight and deep into her soul.

"Crazy . . ." The words were sad and sweet, Cline's voice filled with a sadness and resignation heartbreaking to hear.

Nell was trembling now, listening with closed eyes, and she looked as if she were experiencing a sharp but delicious pain, each note a dart.

"Worry . . ." began the second verse. Nell continued to tremble until the end of the verse.

The last note was long and sustained, a sad cry. It was too much for Nell. She clapped her hands over her ears, desperately attempting to shut out the intense experience, an experience too acute for her to bear.

"Oh . . . Crazy . . ."

Nell ran, driven away by the sound, as if the music were a scourge on her back. A second later the cabin door slammed shut as she sought refuge from the overwhelming sensation in the gloom of her bedroom.

The music shut off abruptly as Olsen hit the stop button on the stereo. Lovell just stared at the cabin, hoping Nell would reappear. No light showed at the window and he could imagine her within, crouched in a corner, wary and watchful, trying to make sense of what she had heard, attempting to sort out the jumble of sensation and emotion that the music had exposed.

"Jesus," he whispered.

"That was my mistake," said Olsen curtly. She had become the psychologist again. "I guess she's never heard music before. She's got no resistance."

Lovell remembered the effect of the same song on Annie. She had lacked resistance too, but of a different sort. "That's not weakness," he said. "That's a gift."

FIFTEEN

It was a different Paula Olsen who strode into the conference room in the psychiatric wing of the Washington State Medical Facility. Her outward appearance was little changed, save for the smart suit she wore and the expensive briefcase she carried, but her attitude toward Nell and Jerry Lovell had been altered considerably.

Professor Paley was still her mentor and guide, but she was determined not to be pressured into hasty conclusions or intemperate decisions regarding Nell's future. Paula still considered herself on the team—she just wished the team did not include Goppel and Malinowski. It wasn't that she didn't respect their opinions or professional expertise—rather it was that she was beginning to feel that the more people involved, the more likely Nell's well-being would be compromised.

She was flabbergasted to find not three people waiting for her in the conference room but nine—Paley, Goppel, and Malinowski had been joined by six more and they were some of the most prominent names in psychology.

"Come in, Paula, come in," said Paley, ushering her into the room. He had the air of a man who had just sprung a surprise party on the startled birthday girl.

Paula looked around the room and managed a weak smile.

Paley did the introductions. "This is Louis Gottschalk from the National Institute of Mental Health . . . Jim Oleson and Judith Lazorek, Harvard Neurological Institute . . ."

Paula nodded at each, her head bobbing like a puppet, and was sure she looked like an idiot.

"Ben Rosa, who is with the Hersheim at Stanford," Paley continued. "Ralph Harris, associate editor of the *Journal of Autism and Childhood Schizophrenia*. Anniko Morishima, whose work of course you know . . ."

Slightly dazed by the academic firepower, Paula dropped into a seat at the table. She busied herself with the notes and papers in her briefcase, buying a little time, organizing her thoughts. The first thing she realized was that there was more going on here than Paley calling in some heavy-hitting backup to assist in Nell's diagnosis and therapy. This array of luminaries was a vote of confidence in Paula, her skills, in the importance of Nell. Olsen was grateful for that—but there was more and she didn't like it at all.

Paley was sending her a message—two messages, really. The first was about Paley himself. He was underscoring his power, telling her not to question his authority. Only Alexander Paley could summon up powerful friends and colleagues, eminent men and women from the best institutions in the world prepared to fly across the country at his request.

The second message was about Paula. Paley was showing her the glittering prizes, the kind of distinction and prestige she could expect to attain.

Academic careers are built not just on research and

inquiry, but through a network of friends and protectors and any one of the men or women at that table would be a valuable ally; the National Institute of Mental Health, the Harvard Neurological Institute, and the Hersheim Institute would be prestigious places to begin her rise in the academic ranks; a timely article in the *Journal of Autism and Childhood Schizophrenia* would ensure that rise. All of this could be Paula Olsen's for the taking— but only if she did as she was told and toed the Paley line.

Paley beamed happily at his array of dignitaries. "Ladies and gentlemen," he said genially, "I believe we have been presented with a unique opportunity to study the process of human development under controlled conditions . . ."

Paula frowned. She didn't like the sound of that ominous term "controlled conditions."

Paley did not notice his junior colleague's uneasiness. "In a moment I shall ask Paula Olsen to speak. But first, the star of our show—Nell."

He pressed the remote control in his hand and the large, wall-mounted TV screen buzzed with a snarl of static, then the images sorted themselves out and Nell appeared on the TV screen. She was staring directly into the lens of the video camera—plainly she had just discovered it.

Slowly she moved closer to it, paused, and then moved closer still. Her eyes were intent and filled with curiosity and puzzlement. Olsen could see that Nell was thinking and looking, summoning up the courage to move nearer. When she did she was so close that she was breathing on the lens, the screen misting over.

During the few short seconds Nell's image was obscured, Paula looked around the table. All nine people were leaning forward in their chairs, hardly breathing. Not one blinked, their eyes fixed on the screen. Paula

Olsen smiled to herself—Nell had once again worked her magic.

Lovell was asleep and dreaming. He had consumed most of the bottle of wine the night before and he was snoozing soundly as a result. His sleep, however, was not completely untroubled. Something was buzzing—literally—in his brain, an insistent hum droning through his dreams. The confused and chimerical clutter of images and situations were baffling, a weird amalgam of fantasy and reality. Nell was there, so was Paula and Annie—in his dream he felt his heart lift and soar to see her alive and happy—yet behind it all was that constant, unrelenting buzz. Lovell rolled in his sleep and continued to duel with his subconscious.

Nell was awake and she heard the buzz as well. The noise was not unfamiliar to her, yet she was frightened of it only because it was a daytime sound and Nell knew well that bad things were afoot under the sunshine.

She tried to forget the drone, losing herself in the simple but fabulous process of making her breakfast. To others the process of making oatmeal is an uncomplicated, mundane procedure—through Nell's eyes it was nothing short of a miracle. The feathery white flakes falling from the box, passing through the bright shaft of a luminous, dusty sunbeam, and fluttering into the bowl were things of beauty. The cascade of water from the old, dented enamel pitcher caught the sunlight and glittered like a waterfall.

The result was a simple bowl of lumpy rolled oats and water mixed in a cracked porcelain bowl. It was Nell's staple diet, bland and boring, tasted like dust, but under her absorbed attention it became a thing of wonder.

She was seated at the table in the kitchen, hungry for

her breakfast, but she waited a moment, her head bowed in silent prayer, a mute grace.

Then Nell began to eat, dipping a well-worn wooden mixing spoon into the thin gruel and consuming her Spartan breakfast quickly and with a degree of satisfaction. There were no extremes of taste in her diet—no fiery spice or cloying confections—so, in time, she had come to savor the subtle flavors and textures of a bowl of otherwise dull oatmeal. She ate rapidly and with absolute concentration and within a few moments she had emptied her bowl and had scraped out every last scrap.

The buzz was still in the air, whining and obdurate.

Nell put aside her bowl and spoon and sat absolutely still, her attention caught by the ray of sunlight falling across the table. She thrust her hand into the beam, palm open, as if holding the shaft of golden light in her hand. Her eyes were fixed on the sunbeam, watching it, her lips forming half-spoken words, as if she was reliving a memory.

"Ah, si'fu' naish," she murmured. *"Ah peep'u lai'wi' neek'ty, ah see' o'eva'dur . . ."*

The drone was growing louder and drawing nearer.

A motorcycle roared through the forest, the howling of the engine filling the air. Billy Fisher, mounted on his dirt bike, roared over the ridge, tearing up the rough terrain around the lake. He hadn't been out that way since Ma Kellty died; he had always enjoyed the rugged ride but hated dealing with the insane, crazy old lady—now that she was gone he could enjoy his excursion without the unpleasant end result.

He wrenched the machine from side to side as he went, heading nowhere in particular. He was merely seeking out embankments to climb and natural ramps to leap. The thick rubber knots on his fat tires kicked up the dirt on the tracks, leaving a heavy cloud of dust hanging in the air.

Rocketing up the side of a steep rise, Billy Fisher brought the bike to a halt in a gritty breaker of dirt and pebbles. He stood at the top of the slope that descended into the clearing, wondering which way to head next when he saw two things that astonished him. One was the motor home looking as out of place as an alien space-craft. The other was Nell.

As Billy stared, the door of the cabin was thrown open with a loud bang and Nell came storming out of the house, a wild, crazed look in her eyes.

She was screaming like a demon, her anguished wails echoing out over the lake. Billy's jaw dropped as he watched, sure that this creature was having a fit. She waved her arms, thrashing like a madwoman, time and again she stamped her feet, the heels of her work boots beating a tattoo on the weathered boards of the porch, like a child throwing a tantrum.

Nell screeched in wrath and indignation. *"Yaah! Hai! Hai! Zzzzzzslit!"* Her wild eyes scanned the clearing as she screamed, as if searching for the fabled *eva'dur*.

"Woah!" gasped Billy. He could feel the hairs on his neck standing stiff at the sound of the ungodly wails.

Then the door of the houseboat flew open and Billy was amazed to see Dr. Lovell come racing out into the clearing. His hair was in disarray and his feet were bare. He was hurriedly buttoning his shirt as he ran.

"Nell! What happened? What is it?"

"Gone way!" Nell screamed. "Gone way!" She seized Lovell's hand and started dragging him into the cabin.

Billy Fisher was scared—he was sure that this wild woman was freaking out because he was on the property. He kicked the engine of his bike into life and peeled out, shooting away from the terrifying scene, his mind reeling. A crazy woman! Billy figured there must be something cursed about that cabin—first Ma Kellty, now this ranting wild woman!

"No one is gonna believe this," he shouted into the wind. "Nobody!"

Nell kicked and beat at the table in the kitchen, thrashing and flailing, screaming at the top of her voice. *"Wor'i'a law! Gone way! Gone way!"*

Lovell had not seen her this upset since the first days after the discovery. Her hands were curved into claws and she lacerated the air around her, keeping him at bay. Lovell felt sick at heart, as if a patient who appeared to be nicely on the mend had suffered a massive relapse.

"Nell, *please* . . ." He could make little sense of her frenzied words. *"Gone way"* was clear enough, but what was *"wor'i'a law"*?

Nell kicked madly at the table, smashing her boot into the shelf underneath, the table jumping with every jolt.

"What's gone away, Nell?" he asked, his voice as calm as he could make it.

She continued to kick, but this time she pointed furiously. *"Wor'i'a law! Gone way!"*

Suddenly it all came clear. The shelf under the table was where he had discovered the sheaf of legal papers belonging to Violet Kellty—along with the family Bible.

"Wor'i'a law!" Nell screamed.

"Word of the Lord," said Lovell. "Nell, wait here. I'll go get it."

He sprinted back across the clearing, virtually throwing himself into the houseboat's cabin. Paula Olsen had all of her notes, the audiotapes and videocassettes and her reference works carefully arranged and catalogued in three cardboard file boxes. Lovell fell on them and began ransacking the meticulously kept records. In the few short minutes it took for him to locate the Bible, he reduced her carefully arranged inventory to a chaotic ruin. He didn't care. Right then the most important thing was to put Nell at ease.

The effect of the Bible on Nell was remarkable and immediate. The instant he returned to the kitchen, she snatched the book from Lovell's outstretched hands and clutched it to her breast. Her panic vanished at once and she rocked back and forth, swaying gently and hugging the Bible the way a child snuggles a beloved cuddly toy.

She smiled and looked at Lovell, a warm contentment in her eyes. She seemed to think that he had done something heroic in returning her cherished possession to her.

"Maw done spee' Nell wor'i'a law fo she come fearly," she said quietly.

"I'm sorry," said Lovell. "We shouldn't have taken it away from you."

She held out the Bible, offering it to him with a shy, uncertain smile. *"Enja spee Nell?"*

"You want me to read it to you?" He took the Bible from her and the book fell open at a place where the old spine was cracked. It was the beginning of the Book of Isaiah, the fourth verse of the first chapter underscored in heavy black pencil.

"Ah sinful nation—" he began slowly. As he read, Nell spoke along with him, from memory, matching him word for word.

"Ah si'fu' naish—"

"A people laden with iniquity—"

"A peep'u lai' wi' neekty—"

"A seed of evildoers—"

"A see' o'eva'dur—"

He looked up, their eyes locked together. *"Eva'dur* . . . Evildoer," he said. Eight lines of the Bible had become Nell's Rosetta Stone, the key not just to her language but to her fears and torments.

"Eva'dur," said Lovell. "Show me *eva'dur*, Nell."

She was reluctant, as if acting it out would release it. *"Eva'dur done yow Nell, reckon."*

"Show me."

Nell swallowed hard and then screwed her features into a fierce rictus, like a scream frozen on her face. She bellowed like a wild beast. Then she reached out to take Lovell in her arm, licking her lips and rolling her eyes.

"Eva'dur done hol' inna rass," she said. *"Done come lilt, lilt an hai!*

"Zzzzzslit!" Without warning Nell punched Lovell square in the belly. He was taken completely by surprise and there was enough force behind the blow to wind him mildly. More surprising than the blow was the look on Nell's face. It was a gross, exaggerated pantomime of . . . lust.

"The *eva'dur* hits you like this?" Lovell took Nell's fist, drew it out, and made her fist strike him again. He wanted to be sure he understood what she was telling him.

Nell stared at him in silence, the knuckles of her fist still pressing against the muscles of his belly. Then her eyes widened and her voice dropped to a whisper.

"Skoo' inna belly," she said.

"Skoo'?"

"Skoo'a."

Nell picked up a kitchen knife from the table and held it point first toward her navel, the blade pointing out horizontally. Lovell stared. The picture was becoming clear. Violet Kellty, traumatized by sex, by men, had passed on her sketchy knowledge of sex and her hatred of it to her daughter. Beyond the door lived the evildoers, men crazed by lust, who only wanted women for a single, painful, shameful purpose.

Paula returned to the clearing at dusk. Lovell was waiting for her, sitting on the forward deck of the houseboat. He looked her over, taking in the details of her suit, her high heels, and the briefcase. She looked like a wealthy young stockbroker just arriving at her country house after a grueling week at the office.

"How was the market today?" he asked with a wry smile. "Or did you go on a job interview."

Olsen pulled a heavy carton of supplies from the tiny trunk of the sports car. He had no idea how close to the truth he actually was. "Please," she said. "I'm tired. It's been a very long day."

Lovell took the box from her and Olsen pulled off her high heels and walked in her stocking feet to the door of the houseboat. "So, tell me what I missed," she said.

"You missed a big one. Another breakthrough."

"Damn . . . What the *hell* happened here?" She surveyed the wreckage in her tiny living room. Lovell was surprised—*he* thought he had done a pretty good job of cleaning up.

"Nell needed her Bible," he said. "In fact, she needed it in a hurry."

"Why?" Paula pulled two cans of beer from the miniature refrigerator and tossed one to Lovell.

"She discovered it was missing and she got upset." He popped the tab and took a swig.

"That's the breakthrough?"

Lovell shook his head. "Just the beginning. I found out what Nell is so afraid of. I unlocked the secret of the *eva'durs*."

"Huh . . . That could be a breakthrough. So tell me, who are they?"

"*Eva'durs* are evildoers. And Nell has been told that the people who do evil are wicked men."

"Is there another kind? Seems to me Nell has learned a very valuable lesson."

"Very funny . . . But to Nell there is no man who isn't evil. My guess is she's been told that all men are

136

monsters. If you looked at the world through Violet Kellty's eyes that would make a lot of sense."

"To Nell all men are monsters," said Olsen. "Except you. Is that it?"

Lovell grinned. "I'm not a man," he said.

"You're not?"

"Uh-uh." He shook his head. "Haven't you heard? I'm Jerry *ga'inja*. I'm an angel."

Olsen burst into laughter. "Well," she said, "at least we know she has a sense of humor."

SIXTEEN

Nell's humming was low and peaceful and she rocked gently on her bed, the shadow of a smile on her lips. Lovell and Olsen talked as they watched her on the monitor. Paula was taking notes, glancing at the screen, then down at her notebook, like an artist sketching a model. Lovell observed and thought.

It had been a roller-coaster day for Nell, she had reeled from intense agitation to profound trust, but now she seemed calm and relaxed, the emotional extremes having left no apparent scars on her. But Lovell knew they were there, just below the surface, a constant source of pain.

"Suppose your only close encounter with men was terrifying violence. Rape," he said. "You'd tell your daughter that all men were monsters, wouldn't you? That would be Violet Kellty's perspective, wouldn't it?"

Olsen nodded. "Uh-huh. That would make sense. That kind of trauma is almost impossible to eradicate. With therapy the effects can be controlled . . ." She smiled wryly. "But Violet Kellty didn't sound like much of a candidate for therapy, did she?"

"No. I think that she wanted to protect Nell. Violet would want to warn her about what men could do to you. I think Violet told Nell about rape. I bet she drummed it into her until Nell was so terrified she couldn't even think of the world beyond the cabin without getting hysterical."

Olsen looked up from her notes and gazed at Nell for a moment. "Told her? How?"

"Well, Violet was a little vague on the process. She said, *'Skoo'inna belly.'"*

"Which means?" Olsen turned to her word list.

"Knife in the belly." He put his hand to his crotch. "The knife comes out here."

"Nell told you that?"

"Yes."

"You think she's ever seen it?" Olsen asked.

"The real thing? No. I don't see how she could. Violet wouldn't let her out, no one knew she was here."

Lovell could see that Olsen was thinking fast. "It could be all that's keeping her from coming out in daytime. A deliberately implanted phobia."

"But that doesn't make sense. Why is she more likely to be raped in daytime?"

"She isn't," said Olsen. "But she's more likely to be seen in daytime. And Violet didn't want anyone to see Nell. She was the ultimate mother hen, desperate to protect her daughter against the same terror she had undergone, even if that meant hiding Nell here for her entire life."

"Yeah," said Lovell, glancing at the screen. "I buy that." He wondered who the rapist was, if he was still alive, and if he had any conception of the torment he had caused in two innocent lives. A flash of anger flared in his belly.

140

"The usual treatment for phobias is exposure to the focus of that fear," said Olsen. "And for that we need to find someone she trusts. Someone she trusts who just happens to be a man." She smiled sweetly.

"Exposure to the focus of the fear . . . ?" Lovell realized what she was getting at. "You mean you want me to . . ." Lovell blushed faintly. "Hey. Hey. Not so fast."

"Such modesty . . . Don't you want to help?" she asked innocently.

"Well, of course, but—"

Olsen cocked her head. "This is one job you're better equipped to perform. I thought you'd like to take an opportunity to really shine."

"Oh, I get it," said Lovell sardonically, "you want me to walk over there, pull down my pants, and show her my—"

"No, of course not," Olsen said quickly.

"That's good, because I can't think of a better way to get her to run screaming into the woods. We'd never see her again and I'd go from being *ga'inja* to *eva'dur* in a heartbeat."

"I had no idea it was so impressive," said Olsen.

Lovell laughed. "They say size doesn't matter."

"And it doesn't. Particularly not in this case. But it would be a simple matter to . . . *insinuate* it into her consciousness, her understanding."

"*Really?* I can't wait to find out how you think I should break the ice."

"Simple," said Olsen. "Just wait until tonight. When she goes swimming."

Not long after dusk turned to night, Paula and Jerry watched from the shadows as Nell came out of the cabin and without a glance toward the houseboat walked to the jetty. She shed her clothes and dove into the water, disappearing beneath the waves with hardly a splash.

"I believe that's your cue," Olsen whispered.

Lovell took her hand and pulled her toward the jetty. "Come on," he said. "I want you right there beside me." Lovell wore nothing but a pair of shorts.

"You want a chaperon?"

"For the record."

Together they sat on the edge of the pier and watched as Nell gamboled and romped in the dark water. She did not seem surprised to see them. It was the first time that they had approached her while she was swimming, but she showed no fear or shyness about her nakedness. She flipped in the water like a fish and started swimming back toward them, glowing with the shock of the cold night water.

Olsen nudged Lovell in the ribs. "Now is as good a time as any."

He swallowed hard. "Do I warn her?"

"Just do it. Act like it's no big deal."

Lovell chuckled. "Believe me, it *is* no big deal." He eased off his shorts and sat fully naked on the end of the jetty, his legs dangling, his toes just touching the chilly water.

Nell was standing in the water, chest deep, watching curiously. She started at Jerry's face, then ran her eyes down his body, across his bare chest, her gaze coming to rest in his crotch. It seemed to take a moment or two for her to actually focus on his penis, but when she realized what she was looking at, her mouth dropped open and she stared in surprise. Then she looked up at Paula Olsen and pointed, eager to share her amazing discovery.

"Loo', Pau'a! Missa pogie!"

Olsen grinned and laughed. "Yes, Nell. I know."

Lovell slipped into the water, shivering at the jolt as the frigid water hit his warm skin. The water came up to

142

his waist, but Nell continued to stare, looking into the water like a fisherman.

"Nay tata, missa chickabee. We inna tye'a fellis, yo'kay?" She spoke softly, as if trying to calm a small, frightened wild animal.

Then, for the first time, it struck Nell that Lovell's body was different from her own. Nell reached out and placed a soft hand on the hard plate of his chest, then on his nipple, stroking the wiry hair surrounding it. From there her hand explored farther, crawling up his neck to his jaw, tracing the line, kneading the stubble of his beard.

Paula Olsen watched this silent exploration and, with a sudden shock, realized that she too was rediscovering the otherness, the beauty of the male body.

Nell turned to her, her eyes wide with wonder.

"It's called a man, Nell."

"Man," said Nell.

"He won't hurt you."

As if looking to him for confirmation, she turned back to Lovell. He met her gaze, feeling awkward but determined to stand his ground.

"Thou ar'beau'fu', o ma' love, as Tirzah." Neither Lovell nor Olsen recognized that the line was from the Song of Solomon.

Her hand strayed from his jaw to his cheek, stroking him there, using the gesture he had seen many times before. Aware that this was some kind of statement of trust, he lifted his own hand to her cheek and attempted to mimic the gesture.

Nell's eyes filled with happiness and she twisted and curled under his fingers like a cat. Then she threw herself into his arms and held him tight, her head burrowing into the hollow of his neck. Lovell felt the warmth of her body against his and instinctively enfolded her in a strong embrace.

Paula Olsen felt a sudden stab of jealousy, a pang sharp and deep.

As if waking from a dream, Nell started and pulled herself free of his embrace, then darted away in the water like a fish. Lovell watched her go, but he could feel the place on his back where her hands had touched like a burn.

SEVENTEEN

"Some people would say that was unethical," said Lovell.

He was fully dressed now and toweling his hair dry. Olsen had retrieved a bottle of wine from her refrigerator and was engaged in opening it.

"I was rather impressed," she said as she wrestled with the cork. "I couldn't have done that."

Lovell dropped into one of the lawn chairs under the canvas canopy and exhaled heavily. He tried to act nonchalant about his encounter with Nell, but Paula could see that the experience had been an emotional one. He seemed tired, drained.

Paula extracted the cork and poured him a glass of wine. "It took courage."

"More than you know," Lovell said with a weary smile. "When I was younger, I used to really hate it when anyone saw me naked. When I spent the night with a girl, I'd wait till she went to the bathroom and then I'd strip off and get into bed."

"I *still* do that. I was sure I was the only one."

"Far from it." They both laughed. Any experience they shared now seemed sweeter, more potent in the light of the animosity that had existed between them so recently.

"How is it that in the movies they never have a problem getting their clothes off?" She took a sip of her wine. "It doesn't seem to bother them at all."

"They do it with their clothes on."

"And on the kitchen table. Like Michael Douglas and Glenn Close in *Fatal Attraction*."

Lovell was quick to correct her. "No, that was the kitchen sink. The kitchen table . . . You're thinking of Jack Nicolson and Jessica Lange. *The Postman Always Rings Twice*."

"You're an expert on sex scenes?" Olsen asked.

"Just an enthusiastic amateur."

"Have you ever seen a sex scene in a movie that you really believed?"

Lovell nodded vigorously. "Absolutely."

"Like which?"

"Debra Winger and Richard Gere in *An Officer and a Gentleman*. Kathleen Turner and William Hunt in *Body Heat*."

"There's only one I've ever believed. Julie Christie and Donald Sutherland in *Don't Look Now*. Remember that one? I believed that."

"Well that was easy," he said knowingly. "They were having an affair when that movie was being made."

Olsen shook her head. "No, that's not it. You know what was so great about that scene. They were married. That was hot marital sex."

"You married?"

"Do I act like I'm married?"

"You might have been married once," Lovell said with a shrug. It was the kind of gesture that said "anything is possible."

"No," Olsen said with exaggerated mock solemnity. "I am not now nor have I ever been married."

"You seeing somebody?"

"No."

"Why not?"

"What's it to do with you?" she asked sharply. Olsen wasn't being playful now.

Lovell backed down immediately. "Okay. Sorry."

"Are *you* married?"

Lovell nodded. "I was."

His marriage had fallen apart after the death of Annie. His depression had been dark and profound and he had been hell to live with. His wife had tried to bring him out of it, but he had been recalcitrant, stubbornly resisting any attempts to alleviate his gloom. He could hardly blame his wife for leaving him, but it had only added to his burden of guilt.

"Are you seeing somebody?"

"No."

"Why not?"

"I guess it just hasn't happened."

"There you go," said Olsen. "The ones you want, you can't get. The ones you get, you don't want. You have Lovell's law—that's Olsen's law."

"So Nell's well out of it, I guess," said Lovell. He reached for the wine bottle. "Lucky break for her. Maybe her only break, right?"

"You mean, she's lucky to miss out on sex? Or on love?"

Lovell shook his head. "Not love. Nell knows all about love. That's for sure." He traced Nell's stroking gesture in the air. "You know when she does this—"

"She's saying I love you."

"That's my guess too." Lovell was pleased that they were beginning to see eye to eye.

"So she is capable of profound love and yet you still think she's well out of sex?"

"I don't think she knows anything about it. Beyond *'skoo inna belly,'* which isn't exactly the most level-headed view. And I couldn't begin to think of how to change her thinking."

"You did okay in the water."

"You're not suggesting—"

"Of course not." Olsen laughed as he shifted uncomfortably. "I'm just saying you managed to finesse the first step pretty easily. That's all."

"All she learned was that there was a difference between men and women. Sex remains an unknown quantity."

"Well . . . She's going to have to learn someday."

Billy Fisher was seven beers into his evening's entertainment at Frank's Bar. Things were shifting into high gear—he wasn't drunk enough to be comatose, but he had put away more than enough alcohol to make him very, very obnoxious.

He was not alone. Joining him at the bar were three of his friends—Jed, Stevie, Shane—and like Billy, they were in their late teens, minimally employed in casual jobs that paid minimum wage. None of them held out much hope for the future, so they found refuge in immoderate beer consumption that led to noise and, if they were lucky, a fight. Beyond that they had little to hold their interest, except for swaggering around Richfield's narrow streets or riding their beat-up motorcycles too fast through pristine mountain terrain.

Had Billy and company bothered to look a few feet to the left they would have gotten a pretty good deal of what their futures ultimately held for them. The only other patrons in the dark, damp bar were a few of the regulars, older men who had started their adult life much like Billy

Fisher and his buddies. There were only eight other men in the bar, five of them were locals, long laid off from the logging and mining industries, now eking out a living on government supplemental income checks and meager pensions. They were folded over their drinks, as if praying for a turn in their luck, pausing only to take a gulp of beer or to glance at the silent Seattle Mariners' game on the TV set above the bar.

The other three men in Frank's were strangers. They were older than Billy and friends, but younger than the old-timers by at least two decades. All of them wore jeans and flannel shirts, hiking boots on their feet, but their country attire belied their city look. Anyone in Richfield who saw them and who bothered to form an opinion about this group would have assumed that they were some guys up from Seattle for a little hiking, camping, and communing with nature—and they would have been dead right.

But Billy Fisher hadn't noticed the strangers or anyone else, for that matter. He slammed his beer mug down on the bar. "Wild woman! Yee-hah!"

"There ain't no wild woman," said Jed wearily.

"I'm telling you, fuck brain, it's the fucking truth." Billy swigged his beer and wiped his mouth with the back of his hand, then emitted a belch as loud as a rifle shot.

Either the vehemence of Billy's words or the vigor of the belch seemed to impress Jed. "You seen her? You seen this wild woman, Billy?"

"Sure, I've seen her."

"Yeah?" Stevie challenged. "What's so goddam wild about this woman."

Insightful description was not Billy's strong suit. He shrugged. "She's just wild. Like an animal."

"So she got no clothes, right?" said Shane with a leer.

"Can't be wild and be wearin' clothes. A wild woman gotta be buck naked, right?"

Jed seemed to get caught up in the spirit of the fun. "Not buck naked, Shane. *Fuck* naked! Runnin' around the forest fuck naked!"

"Wild woman!" Shane bellowed. "Yee-hah! You think she fucks like a dog?" He turned his face to the low-hung ceiling and bayed. "Roowf! Roowf!" His hips bucked and pumped against the bar, humping the worn wood like a dog on a bitch.

"Wild woman!" yelled Billy Fisher.

His companions picked up the call.

"Wild woman! Yee-hah! Rowf! Rowf!"

The locals in the bar were used to this rowdiness but they knew that if they complained they would just be playing into Billy's hands. Objections would just lead to an endless argument that could escalate into fisticuffs. So the old men just looked disgusted and went on drinking, pretending to be so engrossed in the ball game that they hadn't even heard the ruckus the boys kicked up.

The three strangers, by contrast, looked amused by this display of rustic high spirits. One of them stood up and walked over to the bad boys.

"Hi there," he said affably.

Billy, Shane, Jed, and Steve stopped their howling and glared at him.

"What do you want?" Billy growled.

"You say you've found a wild woman in the forest?"

His buddies were watching him, so Billy did his best to cop an attitude and look defiant. "What if I have?"

"I'd be interested," said the outsider. "Tell me about her."

Even a boy as dim as Billy could see that there was something here he could exploit to his advantage. "Maybe, I will, maybe I won't," he said slyly.

The stranger slid onto a bar stool and signaled to Frank the bartender. "How about a round here."

"That's better." Billy grinned as Frank set up five cold bottles of beer. Free drinks were very few and far between in a bar like Frank's. "Who the hell are you, anyhow?"

The man flipped open his wallet and pushed a business card across the bar. Billy picked it up and squinted at it, but the stranger translated for him.

"Mike Ibarra," he said. "Seattle *Times*. I'm a journalist."

EIGHTEEN

Had it not been for his status as her friend, not to mention being an angel, Nell would have thought that Jerry Lovell had lost his reason. He was seated on her porch, facing her, his tongue stuck straight out of his mouth. Nell watched him for a moment, then pushed out her tongue, as if in retaliation.

It wasn't easy for Lovell to talk around his outthrust tongue. "Okay. Watch this."

He pulled a kernel of caramel popcorn from the bag on the table in front of him and placed the sweet little nugget in the middle of his tongue and then sucked it into his mouth.

"Hmmm," he said, rolling his eyes. "Sweet . . ." He swallowed the popcorn and licked his lips. "Okay," he said. "Now it's your turn."

Nell's tongue still hung out of her mouth. He dropped a piece of popcorn on it. "Eat it," he urged. "It's good."

Nell wasn't so sure. Her eyes swiveled in their sockets

and she went cross-eyed as she strained to see the morsel resting on her tongue.

"You'll like it," said Lovell. "Go on . . ."

She pulled her tongue back into her mouth, holding the corn there, as if trying to prevent it touching the inside of her cheeks. But as the popcorn melted, the sweetness hit her taste buds and she gasped sharply, almost overcome by the intense, exquisite sensation. It was the first thing she had ever tasted, beyond the tedious gruel and the occasional glass of fresh milk. Her eyes lit up with pleasure. And then out came her tongue, ready for more.

"See. I told you you'd like it." But he wasn't prepared to give her any more popcorn—not, that is, until he got something in return.

Lovell got up from the table and walked backward to the top step and then held out his hand, showing her the treat.

Nell followed, her tongue still out, stopping just shy of him, but Lovell rewarded her with some popcorn nonetheless.

"Okay. So far, so good." Lovell walked down the three steps to the ground and then stopped. "Come on, Nell," he coaxed. "Come down and get some more." He held out a whole handful of popcorn enticingly.

But Nell stayed where she was, parked at the head of the steps. He could see that she was yearning for more popcorn, like a small child she was craving it with all her body and soul. She glanced around the clearing, peering suspiciously at the bright light of day.

"Nobody is going to hurt you," said Lovell. "Come down and get some more."

"Kine'ey Je'y. Kine'ey, kine'ey Je'y," she whined. Nell capered and jumped, stamping her foot like a little girl. *"Ooo-oooooh! Wanna-wanna-wanna-wanna."*

"Come and get it."

Nell looked longingly. Then, suddenly, she gathered

up all her courage and dashed into the clearing, skidded to a halt, and pounced on Jerry. She dug a fistful of popcorn out of the bag, then dashed back to the safety of the steps. Throwing herself down on the boards of the porch, Nell stuffed the popcorn into her mouth and chomped away. Her cheeks were flushed and her heart was pounding, but Lovell was pleased to see that she would risk an encounter with the daylight evildoers to indulge her newfound passion.

"See," he said. "No *eva'durs* out here. Only me."

Nell swallowed hard and licked her lips, hungry for more. Her eyes followed Lovell's every move.

"Okay, now we're going to try something a little different." Lovell placed a mound of popcorn on the grass a few feet from the lowest step, turned, walked a few yards, and put down another. He did this all along the path leading to the water's edge. Then he sat on the step and waited.

It took a while, but Nell did creep away from her sanctuary, away from the security of the cabin, pausing to scoop up the sweet little treasures. Each time she stopped, her head swiveled quickly, left and right, looking around like a wary animal, before she knelt.

Standing in the middle of the track she munched the popcorn, eyeing the next heap, wondering if she had the courage to advance a few more feet to retrieve it.

Lovell and Olsen watched closely for the half an hour it took for Nell to work her way along the path to the water. She moved a little faster as she neared the far end of the track, like a tightrope walker edging toward safety.

Lovell watched the satisfaction, pleased that his simple plan had worked so well. "What'd I tell you? It's got her out of that cabin."

"This is the easy part," said Olsen. "It's *keeping* her out that's going to be hard."

"She's having a good time. She's discovered popcorn. Now she can go to the movies."

Nell had never approached so close to the boat before and she had the sense that she had passed out of her own territory into the domain of outsiders. She lingered a few feet outside the circle, smiling happily and chewing the last of the popcorn. But she was shy and diffident, as if not quite sure of the warmth of her welcome.

"Nay tata, reckon?" asked Lovell.

Nell shook her head. She wasn't afraid anymore, but she was plainly amazed that she had finally managed to venture out of the cabin and into daylight for the first time.

"Shie alo'lay," she said. She looked up, caught sight of the bright sun high in the sky, and raised her arms as if to embrace it. She spun in place, twirling in sure joy. Then she started singing, her voice high and happy.

"Crazy . . . A crazy fo' fee'in' so lone'ey . . . Ah crazy, crazy fo fee'in so blue . . ." Nell had a light, silvery singing voice—but it was her perfect recall of the song that she had heard only once that was so incredible.

"That is amazing," said Lovell. "She remembers every word. Every last one."

"Exceptional memory feats are sometimes a feature of autism in adolescents and adults," said Olsen.

Lovell laughed. "Get off it, Paula. Don't be an academic, for once."

Olsen smiled sheepishly. "I can't help it. You're right. I'm sorry."

"Crazy . . ." Nell sang. "Ah crazy fo' thi'kin I co'ho you . . ."

"She likes it so much," said Olsen. "The music means so much to her."

"If she likes this. Just wait until she hears—" He dove into the houseboat and returned a moment later with the compact disc player. "This!"

He slapped the CD into the machine and in a few seconds Roy Orbison's voice pumped out of the speaker.

Nell spun and whirled with the music, intoxicated by all the new sensations, overcome by the light and space and melody as well as the sweetness lingering on her tongue. Lovell and Olsen watched like proud parents as Nell spiraled away across the clearing. All thoughts of danger and threat under the sun vanished and she danced joyfully.

Roy Orbison's voice filled the air.

Nell closed her eyes. The sunlight seemed to intensify, blazing through her eyelids in a burst of colors; the music grew louder and filled her head. Olsen and Lovell ceased to exist.

And in her mind Nell could see the twin girls. They were spinning together, arms entwined, gazing rapt into each other's eyes, the song carrying them away.

Through the eyes of Olsen and Lovell, Nell appeared to be lost in the haze of the music. She twirled and whirled, frolicking in step with the beat, spiraling back along the path. They looked away for a moment, just long enough to share a proud and proprietary glance. When they looked for her again, the music had played out, Roy Orbison's voice dying away, hanging for a moment in the air.

Lovell looked and blinked. "Where'd she go?"

As if carried away by the fading strains of the song, Nell had vanished.

NINETEEN

Without pausing to think about it, Jerry Lovell began to run, charging into the underbrush, chasing after Nell. Olsen was there too and together they crashed through the woods, running blind. They were well aware that Nell knew her way through the forest, but in the daylight they thought they had more of a chance of catching her.

But somehow she eluded them once again. They had climbed to the top of a hill, a slope thick with trees and undergrowth, a rise overlooking the clearing and the lake beyond. Lovell's chest heaved as he panted, gasping for breath.

"Damn! Damn, damn, damn!" He waved his fists, slamming the air around him. Both Olsen and Lovell had developed an intense curiosity about where Nell went on her expeditions into the forest. Olsen told herself that it was an important piece of the Nell puzzle, that until they knew where she went and why, there would be a blank spot in her psychological profile.

Lovell was curious also, but he was more interested in

knowing where she went simply because it would allow him to know her better than he did now. "We've lost her. Dammit!"

"Shhh!" Olsen was peering into the brush, her head down, listening intently. Farther up the slope, some distance away, she heard a sound, the snapping of a branch, followed by the merest flash of white fabric.

"She's up there," she whispered.

"Where?"

"There." Olsen pointed toward the crest of the ridge. "Let's go."

They set off toward the source of the sound, moving more slowly this time in an inexpert attempt at stalking her. It was beginning to dawn on Olsen that Nell just might want them to be able to follow her this time. They knew that she could move through the forest undetected in the dark of the night, yet this time she had left them a clue, given them a helping hand when the trail went cold. It was as if Nell had decided that she was ready to trust them with a great mystery—but one they would have to work to solve.

They were both sweating when they reached the summit of the ridge, the clammy air under the low branches of the pines was close and wet on their damp skin. They had moved far inland from the lake and were looking out over a deep vee in the landscape, a narrow gorge split by a rock-filled mountain stream. This hidden valley was remote—even more isolated than the lake— unspoiled by man, beautiful. A mantle of serenity had settled here, a kind of peace that was almost tangible, a silence so placid it could be heard.

The river was a half a mile below them, yet they could hear the rush of the water clearly—sound could carry a long way on a windless summer day like this one. Lovell cupped his hands around his mouth and shouted.

"Nell!" His voice rolled out into the hush, but there was no answer, not even an echo.

Carefully they began to pick their way down the slope, slipping and falling where they missed their footing on the steep incline, unsure of where they were going. But they moved without urgency, stopping midway down to rest. Lovell looked out at the vast wilderness stretched before them. From where they stood to the edge of the horizon the landscape was a still, silent spectacle of pines unbroken by a road or a building. There was a feeling in the air, a sensation that no outsider had ever seen this place before.

"This is crazy. She could be anywhere." Something about the panorama made Lovell lower his voice almost to a whisper.

"No. She's here."

"How do you know? What makes you so sure?"

"If she was still moving we'd hear her . . ." She smiled slightly. "Besides, she wants us here."

"*Wants* us here?"

Olsen nodded. "She let us see her. She didn't have to do that."

"Then where is she *now*? I think it would be better to go back to the cabin and wait for her."

Paula sighed and shrugged, reluctant to give up having come so far, but she turned with Lovell and together they headed back up the hillside.

Nell was there, standing motionless between the trees, seeming to have appeared from nowhere. They had passed the spot where she now stood a few moments before and had seen nothing, no trace of her at all. She held a bunch of wildflowers in her hand.

"Je'y done come loo' Mi'i, reckon?"

Lovell was about to reply, but Olsen stopped him, stepping in front of him just as he opened his mouth. "Where's 'me,' Nell? Show us where me is."

161

"Mi'i inna missa feliss."

Olsen looked puzzled. "What did she say?" Lovell was the more fluent speaker of Nell's language.

"Uh . . . I guess it's something like, 'me is in a happy place.' I think."

"What happy place, Nell? Please show us."

Nell nodded and slipped back between the trees. She was moving quickly, surefooted on the slope, and for a moment Lovell and Olsen thought that she was running away, trying to leave them behind. But after she had traveled a few yards she stopped and looked over her shoulder, as if inviting them to follow her.

At the point where the ridge was steepest, Nell vanished again, but this time she slipped through a cleft in the hillside, a foliage-covered crack in the living rock. The crevice was high and narrow and it wasn't easy for a man of Lovell's size to squeeze through, but he forced himself in, the hard rock tearing his clothes.

Once within the fissure widened, opening up. It was pitch-dark inside, but Lovell could sense that he was inside some kind of cave, a deep cut in the rock.

"Nell?" His voice bounced off the walls to the cavern. Paula Olsen was scrambling through the opening and she stood next to him, both waiting till their eyes adjusted to the darkness.

Nell was kneeling next to the inner wall of the cave where the shifting primeval rock had opened a long horizontal crack forming a natural shelf.

"Chicka Mi'i. Lilten, lilten aw tye." Nell's voice was low and calm.

Their night blindness had melted away enough for them to make out the object that brought Nell to this place. Laid out on a natural shelf in the rock, as if in a catacomb, was a skeleton, complete and at rest, but small, the remains of a child.

"My God," gasped Olsen.

162

In the eye sockets of the skull, Nell had laid the heads of the wildflowers, white petals and gold centers. They looked shockingly like eyes.

Olsen and Lovell gazed in silence, not quite sure what to make of this bizarre sight. Nell seemed entirely at ease in the presence of the skeleton, reaching out and stroking the dry bones of the skull's cheek.

"Chicka Mi'i," she said.

Lovell tried to follow her enunication to the letter. *"Mi'i."*

Nell smiled brightly. *"Mi'i done waw wi'a law."*

"Mi'i walks with the Lord," Lovell translated.

"Mi'i feliss aw tye." Nell looked to Lovell for confirmation. *"Reckon?"*

"Reckon," he said with a nod.

Nell turned back to the skeleton, gazing down at it, stroking the gaunt cheekbone, like a mother comforting a sleeping child. It was apparent that for Nell the skeleton was still a living person, a human being with whom she still had a deep and animate connection. Nell was motionless for a long time, deep in concentration, completely focused on the skeleton. After a while she looked up and smiled again, then started for the cleft in the rock.

After the gloom of the cave, the sun felt warm on their skin, the air refreshing. They blinked in the bright light, then the three of them trooped back through the forest, Nell leading the way, like a family out for a stroll on a Sunday afternoon.

Paula Olsen spent much of the rest of the day combing through her collection of tapes, isolating every instance where Nell was reacting with her own image in the mirror. Until the discovery of the skeleton, Olsen had assumed that Nell had divided herself into two persons, a subjective self and an objective self; that she had displaced one personality, projecting it into the mirror.

One self, her physical form, was Nell. The image in the mirror was another side of her—*Mi'i.*

But it was beginning to appear to her that the truth was simpler than that.

When they returned to the clearing, Nell led them into the cabin as if anxious to show them something. In the bedroom, she opened a chest and pulled out some clothing, old dresses and shoes, garments made for children.

"Two smock dresses," said Paula. "Two jerseys. Two pairs of sandals . . . Twins."

Nell held up one of the dresses and held it to her face, kissing the old, worn material. *"Mi'i."*

"They kept everything," Paula said. "It's kind of creepy."

Nell like the sound of the word. "C'eepy," she repeated.

"No. It's not creepy," said Lovell. He caressed the dress, using Nell's affectionate pantomine. "Nell . . . *Mi'i, reckon?*"

Nell nodded eagerly. *"Mi'i."*

"You think she doesn't understand she's dead?" asked Paula.

Lovell shrugged. "I don't know. She said her twin walks with the Lord. Nell . . . *Mi'i waw wi'a law?*"

Nell gazed at him, her features clouding, and nodded slowly.

"Mi'i done go, fo' aw tye? Mi'i done go, fo' aw tye?" Lovell asked.

Nell started, then she started jerking her head sharply, as if rejecting Jerry Lovell's words.

"Mi'i ress wi' Nell," she said plantively.

"Her twin stays with her," said Lovell. "It's like she never died."

But Nell was backing away from them, reaching for

164

the mirror, her distress rising. *"Mi'i nay go!"* she insisted. *"Mi'i ressa Nell!"*

Lovell did his best to calm her. "Okay, Nell. I'm sorry. I didn't mean to—"

But Nell wouldn't listen to him. Her head was pressed against the looking glass and she was crooning mournfully. Out of the cry came words, repeated again and again.

"Thee'n me and me and thee . . . Thee'n me an me'n thee . . ."

Lovell and Olsen watched, helpless in the face of her grief.

"Mistake," said Lovell. "Sorry. I didn't know."

"She knows," said Olsen. "It's just that she won't let go."

Paula returned to the houseboat and went through the tapes time and again, isolating every reference to "mi'i."

"That skeleton was her sister and Nell has projected her being into the mirror. If she can't have her sister in the flesh, she is, in effect, keeping the child's spirit alive."

On the video screen, Nell was touching her own image in the mirror, stroking the cheek. "Mi'i," she murmured.

Lovell looked at her eyes, the way they almost burned into the glass. "It's her identical twin," he said. "And to Nell she is actually there. Nell can see her—right there on the other side of the mirror."

"Twins make up their own language," Olsen said. "It's really common. It's as if they're on some kind of private mental wavelength."

"She's still talking to her. It's as if she never died," said Lovell. A small part of his heart bled for Nell. Alone in a world she did not understand, she had created a friend, her sister, someone she knew she could trust. "And the name—Mi'i. It's not 'me,' in the sense of herself. It's someone's name. I've noticed that Nell has trouble with l's and m's where they occur in the middle of a word."

"Could be Milly or Mimi . . . ?" said Olsen.

"We'll probably never find out. But she's alive, isn't she?"

Olsen nodded. "You see, Nell lives in a world of her own—literally."

"I'm beginning to realize that."

"I wonder how she died," said Olsen. "It would be helpful if we could get that skeleton into a lab—"

Lovell grimaced. "She would never understand that. To Nell, that would amount to desecration. That cave is a holy place to her. She's probably still upset that her mother—Maw—was taken away from her."

"Well . . . if we're ever going to find out what happened here, we're going to have to upset things a little bit."

Lovell sank into a chair next to Olsen and fixed a hard stare on her face. "I thought we were beginning to think alike," he said. "I thought that we both wanted what's best for Nell. Then you try something like this. I wish you'd make up your mind. Are you friend or foe?"

Olsen felt a flash of anger. "It's not as simple as that and you know it. Nell isn't some kind of endangered species, you know, some rare bird you have to protect."

"Rare? She's one of a kind, for God's sake."

"She's a human being. One of billions."

"She's unique."

Olsen smiled sardonically. "We're all unique, Doctor. Each of us different in our own little way."

"I hate it when you switch into your Ph.D. mode."

"And I hate it when you're in your aging-hippie-everything-is-beautiful mode."

"Okay. Try this one. You attempt to move that skeleton

166

and I'll tie you up in court for the rest of your life. How's that?"

"Damn you, Lovell." She glanced at her watch and then started stuffing notes and videocassettes into her briefcase. "I'm going to be late."

"Late?" Lovell looked puzzled. "No one is ever *late* in Richfield."

"Not here," said Olsen curtly. "Seattle."

Paula Olsen was late, but not very late—she drove at top speed down through the mountains, her progress slowed only by a summer squall, a cloudburst, that hit the highway between Everett and the outskirts of Seattle. She raced through the halls of the hospital and was breathless by the time she made it to Paley's office. She paused a moment to calm herself before opening the door, then walked in.

Paley studied the batch of papers, the notes and field profiles that she had assembled, in silence, listening as Paula took him step by step through the most recent discoveries. It was difficult for her to keep the excitement out of her voice.

"I can't tell without analyzing the skull, but I'd guess that the remains are those of a child, female, somewhere between six and ten years of age."

"Why not examine the skull?" Paley asked, his eyes did not leave the pages spread out in front of him.

"That would be tricky."

"Tricky? Why?"

Olsen thought it best not to mention Jerry Lovell—but she made his argument. "Possible profound trauma to Nell. It could undo all of the trust we have managed to engender thus far. It would be risky right now."

Paley grunted and nodded.

"If the child died between six and ten years of age, we're looking at twenty years at least from the death of the twin to now. For all that time, her linguistic development has been arrested. Maybe her emotional development too."

"A child aged thirty," commented Paley. He continued to riffle through the pages.

"She's my age. I could be her twin."

Paley pushed his glasses to the end of his nose and he looked at her over the tops of the lenses. "Does she interact with you on that level? Is she treating you like a sister?"

"No." She frowned. "In fact, she responds better to Dr. Lovell than to me."

"Him again," growled Paley.

"He's been helpful."

Paley turned his attention back to the notes. "This is very good, Paula. Very good." He flashed her his avuncular smile. "It deserves proper handling . . ."

"And what constitutes 'proper handling.'"

"I'm going to set up a special unit for Nell, on site. I want total control of her environment. I want to monitor every input, every stimulus, every response. No one has ever done that before. You realize that."

"Yes." Olsen wasn't sure she wanted it done now. She had visions of squads of scientists and researchers stomping through Nell's clearing, invading her home without regard to the fragility of her circumstances, both mental and physical. Or worse, Paley might decide to move her, bring Nell into the hospital itself. A stark and vivid image flashed through her mind: Nell confined in one of the drab observation rooms in the institute, subjected to the merciless scrutiny from behind the one-way glass. Paula could imagine the numb and lifeless look in Nell's blue eyes.

Paley was completely unaware of Olsen's misgivings. No matter how vehement his denial, Nell was not a person to him. She was a case study, a fascinating psychological resource he was determined to exploit.

"We'll make a home for her," said Paley, warming to his subject. "A family. Somewhere safe for her to grow up."

"What about Jerry Lovell?"

"What about him?"

"He's pretty attached to Nell."

"All the more reason to get her away from him." He smiled thinly. "Have you found out what derailed his career?"

Olsen hesitated for only a split second before deciding to lie. "No," she said. "It hasn't come up."

"It would be interesting to know what happened. It would tell us something about the kind of man we're dealing with."

Olsen could have told him volumes about the type of man they were dealing with, but decided to hold her tongue.

Paley leaned back in his desk chair. "He's soft, isn't he?" He seemed almost amused, as if he was looking forward to driving Lovell out of Nell's life. "He's a rat that got out of the rat race because he turned out to be a mouse. Something along those lines, would you say?"

"I wouldn't know," Olsen said, tight-lipped. She was beginning to dislike Professor Paley.

TWENTY

Mike Ibarra ditched his car at the beginning of the rough track that led down to the lake and hiked the rest of the way to the clearing, lugging a bag heavy with camera equipment. He climbed the last rise, the lake, the cabin, and the houseboat spread out before him. It was a beautiful place, but not the untamed wasteland that Billy Fisher had sworn it was. Ibarra was beginning to think that there was nothing in this story, that Billy Fisher had made up this tale of a wild woman merely to gain a couple of rounds of drinks for him and his buddies.

Ibarra shook his head as he paused long enough to shoot a few pictures—as far as he knew, wild women did not usually live on houseboats—then trudged down the hillside toward the cabin.

He climbed the porch steps and knocked on the frame of the screen door, peering into the dim interior. "Hello? Anybody home?"

There was no answer from within, the house was silent

and still. He hesitated a moment, then pulled open the screen door and stepped inside.

Ibarra looked at the old-fashioned fittings, the crude furniture. This part, at least, Billy Fisher had gotten right.

"All the comforts of home," he whispered. He took a reporter's notebook from his back pocket and penciled a few quick notes.

While his back was turned, the door leading to Nell's bedroom opened a crack. Ibarra heard the faint creak and he turned to see Nell squinting at him through the narrow gap, a mixture of fear and curiosity showing on her face.

Ibarra tried to hide his surprise. "Hi," he said, smiling brightly. "I knocked but I figured there was no one home. Sorry about barging in like that . . ." He took a step or two closer to Nell, his hand outstretched. "I'm Mike Ibarra. I'm a journalist. Seattle *Times*."

Nell continued to stare, but did not react to his words, she did not move a muscle. Ibarra figured that this must be the wild woman—and while she was not quite what he had been led to expect, she did look distinctly odd. He raised his camera, showing it to her.

"Okay if I take your picture?" He moved a little closer, raising the viewfinder to his face.

As Nell's curiosity got the better of her, she leaned out from behind the door, staring into the lens. She was startled to see herself reflected in the convex eye of the camera. Ibarra focused and pressed the shutter release, the flash exploding and flooding Nell with a shocking wash of bright white light. She jumped back and trembled for a split second watching the red splotches dancing and jumping before her eyes.

Then Nell screamed, a shriek filled with panic and terror. *"Yaah! Hai! Hai! Zzzzzslit!"* She slammed the door and Ibarra could hear her racing around the room, her screams mounting in volume.

It would be difficult to say who was more frightened.

Mike Ibarra backed away from the door. "Hey—no— it's okay," he stammered. "I didn't mean to frighten you . . . Please. Please stop."

His words seem to have the opposite of their desired effect. Nell screamed louder, heedless of Ibarra's entreaties. Then he felt a strong hand on his shoulder. Lovell hauled the journalist out of the cabin and threw him down the steps. Ibarra landed in a heap, his camera and equipment flying. Lovell stood over him like an avenging angel.

"If you hurt her, you're dead, buddy!" Nell's screams still raged inside the house.

Ibarra scrambled to his feet. "I never touched her. All I did was take her photograph."

"Photograph?" Lovell snatched up the camera. "You took her photograph? What are you? Press?"

Ibarra nodded. "Seattle *Times*." As he bent down to dust himself off, Lovell sprung the back of the camera, letting light in to overexpose the film, then clicked it shut.

"Okay," he said, handing the camera back to Ibarra. "I'm sorry. I guess I overreacted."

"No harm done," mumbled Ibarra. "Who are you?"

"I'm her doctor," said Lovell. "Do me a favor, will you? Forget you ever met her." He glanced toward the house. Nell's screaming had abated somewhat. Now her voice was low-pitched, growling a warning to the evildoer. "Please, just forget the whole thing."

Ibarra smiled and held out his hand. "Mike Ibarra."

They shook. "Jerome Lovell."

"It's like this, Dr. Lovell," said Ibarra deliberately. "I'm a newsman. And I have a strong hunch that woman in there could be news."

Lovell peered at him closely. "How did you hear about her, anyway? Don't try and tell me that you just happened to wander out here. Who told you?"

173

"Dr. Lovell, you must have heard about reporters and their sources. We're kind of protective about them."

"C'mon, Mike. This thing isn't a matter of national security."

"Sorry, Doctor."

Lovell was desperate to keep this story out of the newspapers. "If you turn Nell into a news story, then all you'll end up doing is condemning her to the life of a circus freak."

"Not necessarily," Ibarra protested. "The story could be handled in such a way that—"

"Look, if you don't sensationalize it someone else will. You'll ruin her life and for what? A pat on the back from your editor and an attaboy. 'Great story, Mike. Keep 'em coming.' That what you're after?"

Mike Ibarra turned and looked back at the cabin. Nell was standing at the screen door, watching, but tense and ready for flight. "Her name is Nell?"

"Oh, please," said Lovell with a disgusted shake of his head. "Look. There's no story here—no story beyond the opportunity to destroy the life of an innocent woman if you run with the story. Okay?"

"Maybe we can talk about it . . ."

"We've talked about it. Now I wish you'd get the hell out of here."

"This your property?"

"No," said Lovell.

Ibarra shrugged. "Well, in that case, I don't know that you have the authority to run me off."

"You see the effect you have on her. As her doctor, I'm asking you to leave. And if you don't, the sheriff is a pretty good friend of mine . . ."

Ibarra raised his hands, as if in surrender. "Okay. Okay. I'll go . . ." He started toward the path up the ridge.

Lovell watched him go. He had an uneasy feeling he would be seeing him again.

Over the weeks of their enforced togetherness Lovell and Olsen had evolved an informal division of labor, sharing the chores, cooking and cleaning on alternate nights. It was Lovell's turn to cook that night and he stood at the miniature sink in the kitchenette, chopping vegetables for the evening meal. Paula Olsen sat at the dining table studying her lists of words culled from her now extensive collection of audio- and videotapes of Nell.

Neither of them heard the door of the cabin open, nor did they see Nell stealing across the clearing. She crouched in the darkness and gazed at the houseboat, watching Olsen and Lovell, observing their interaction with the same intensity that they watched her. She could half hear their voices though she couldn't understand the words, but she could sense the strain between them— there was tension in the air that night.

"A reporter was here today," said Lovell. He chopped savagely at a pile of parsley.

Olsen looked up from her vocabulary lists, looking alarmed. "A reporter? How on earth did that happen?"

"I don't know. He wouldn't tell me. It's possible that he went through the court records down in Monroe." He stopped chopping and looked critically at Olsen. "The only people who know are Don Fontana, Sheriff Petersen, and my partner, Amy Blanchard." He paused a moment. "And Professor Paley, of course."

You didn't have to be a mind reader to figure out where Lovell was laying the blame for the leak. Olsen shook her head. "You're wrong. Paley knows that publicity would ruin the whole operation. He did not alert the press to this. Believe me."

"Yeah?" He turned back to his chopping. "Well,

175

whoever it was, this guy was from the Seattle *Times*. And he gave Nell one hell of a fright. He scared the hell out of me too, for that matter."

Olsen put down her pen and rubbed her eyes vigorously. "It's going to happen, you know. She's not going to stay our secret forever."

"Why not?" There was an edgy blade of anger in his voice, as if he was blaming Olsen for Nell's dilemma.

"For God's sake, be realistic. People talk. People notice things. Even out here in the boonies. You of all people would know how hard it is to keep a secret in a small town. I wouldn't be surprised if half the town knows that something is going on out here."

"Well," grumbled Lovell. "It's none of their damn business."

"Maybe not . . . But it's a fact of life. It's as simple as that."

Lovell threw down his knife. "I hate it. Why can't she be left alone to live as she damn well pleases!"

"Why can't any of us?" Olsen retorted. "Why should Nell be any different from the rest of the population? Does anybody get left alone? Not even you live as you please. The world is going to intrude eventually."

"Why should Nell be different? Because she *is* different."

"We've been through this," said Olsen wearily. "If only there was some way of protecting her."

"How? We can't build a wall around the entire forest." He swept the chopped parsley off the cutting board and started to peel a yellow onion.

"We could move her," she said. "Set her up in a place where we control access to her. She would be safe, undisturbed. And she would be available for study." It was Professor Paley's idea, of course, and although Paula had her doubts about it, she felt honor bound to at least try to put it into practice.

Lovell regarded her coldly. "Like a psychiatric unit, maybe?"

"So what's your suggestion?" Paula snapped. "Check her into a Holiday Inn?" Lovell's face was twisted into an unpleasant sneer. "This is all Paley's doing, isn't it? You and Paley want to haul her off and lock her up like a lab rat, don't you? I never should have gotten you involved. I would give anything to have the chance to live that day over again."

Olsen felt a sharp twinge of anger, but she did her best to keep her voice low and even-tempered. "I want to help her in any way I can. Tell me a better plan and I'll listen."

Nell was on the deck now, daring to peer in the window, exploring the strange world of Jerry and Paula. The tenor of the voices was beginning to upset her and she trembled slightly at the sound of each angry word.

Lovell hacked the onion into hunks, the knife blade banging on the cutting board. "Every time you drive out of here, every time you go down the mountain, you're running back to Paley and telling him everything that's going on up here." He poured some olive oil into a sauté pan, ignited the burner, and dropped in the chopped onion.

"I've never made a secret of that." Olsen's words were dry and clipped.

"I wonder what you and Paley have cooked up for her." He shook his head slowly and looked mightily disgusted. "You two ought to be ashamed of yourselves."

Paula's self-control snapped. "Don't be so childish! Al Paley is a world-renowned psychologist. You're damn lucky you had the good fortune to hook up with him in the first place."

"Yeah? Look what he got me. You."

Olsen's cheeks turned bright red. "Say what you want about me, but you just remember, Al Paley is the very best man in his field."

"Great." Lovell turned back to his vegetables, cracking a clove of garlic with the handle of the knife. His appetite had vanished. "Then tell him to stay in his fucking field, okay. And I'll stay in mine. And Nell doesn't need him either."

"So who does she need? You?"

"She could do worse," Lovell mumbled.

"Oh, really?" Paula Olsen laughed sarcastically. "What have you got to offer? What's your big plan for Nell? What kind of future can you give her?"

As her voice grew louder, his became softer, more controlled. "I don't plan to manage her future. I don't make plans. That's your game. You and Al. Go play it somewhere else and leave us out of it."

"Oh, it's *us* now, is it? Jerry and Nell. The two of you, living out here in the wilderness. The child-woman and her strong silent protector."

"Shuttup." He had lost interest in cooking now. Throwing aside the knife, he grabbed the cork screw and pulled a bottle of wine—Olsen's wine—out of the refrigerator.

"That's the way you see it, isn't it? The happy couple without a care in the big bad world."

"What would *you* know about happy couples?" Lovell shouted.

"What would *you* know about anything?" Olsen shouted right back.

Nell was frozen in place at the window. She was breathing rapidly, her chest heaving, her heart beating fast. She hated the sound of the sharp, angry words. An agitated whimper broke from her throat, but it could not be heard above the storm of their argument.

"You don't have the balls to handle a grown woman," said Olsen. "So you solve that particular problem by leeching on to Nell. Pathetic!"

"Jesus! You really are a bitch, aren't you?"

178

"And you're too gutless to take responsibility—"

"Listen to you!" Lovell roared. "And *you're* supposed to be the grown woman around here? You're just some girl who wants to please the big daddy back down there in Seattle, that's all you are."

"The hell I am!" Olsen's anger was hot and fierce now. She yelled just as loud as Lovell. "I'm *doing* something, *making* something out of this situation. Not like you. You're so goddamn sensitive. Too sensitive to take a chance, to accomplish a damn thing!"

They were flailing away at each other, hurling words like spears in an attempt to hurt—really hurt—the other. But in the heat of the moment, neither Olsen nor Lovell noticed that each knew the precise weakness of the other. Without realizing it, they had come to know each other too well.

"You want to know your problem?" Lovell snapped. "I'll tell you your goddamned problem—"

She cut him off savagely. "My problem? What about yours? You are too shit scared to do a fucking thing. So worried about putting a foot wrong, so afraid of making a mistake you are fucking paralyzed!"

"And you are afraid of men!"

This observation brought her up short for a moment—but only for a moment. She raised herself to her full height and screamed. "How the hell would you know? You're not a man! You are a fucking blob!"

Without thinking, Lovell grabbed the heavy sauté pan on the stove and raised it as if he was going to club her with it. A shower of onions glistening with a coating of warm golden oil flew around the room.

"Going to hit me now?" Olsen taunted. "Going to kill me? You know about that, don't you? The only fucking decision you've ever taken in your life and you—"

Her words hurt like a stab wound. For a split second Lovell really was afraid that he was going to brain her with the frying pan. It took every ounce of self-control he possessed, but he managed to slam the pan down, not on her head, but on the tabletop. The metal hit the wood with a terrifying crash.

"Goddamn you!" Lovell screamed.

"Aiee!" Suddenly, the door of the cabin was thrown open. Nell stood there, staring at them, a look of profound fear and panic in her eyes. She screeched and whimpered, her head jerking convulsively from side to side. She fell on Lovell and seized his face in her hands, as if trying to stop the flow of angry words. *"Ga'inja spee' wor'i a law!"* she wailed.

Lovell and Olsen were too stunned to move. Nell slowly sunk to her knees, shaking violently and sobbing plaintively. It was a terrifying sound, like that of a child in pain. She pressed her forehead to the floor and cried, as if begging them to stop their arguing. *"Ga'inja . . . Kine'ey ga'inja . . . Ga'inja ressa law . . ."*

In an instant Lovell was on his knees next to her, embracing her, holding her close. He could feel her quivering against him, her heart pounding. "Sure. Sure. *Ga'inja ressa law,"* he whispered. "Everything's okay. Really it is . . ." He glanced at Olsen. "Say something. Make her feel that it's okay."

Olsen smiled faintly and bent down and stroked her hair. "It's okay, Nell. Mommy loves Daddy, really she does. Honest . . ."

It took a while to calm Nell down, but after an hour of soft words and gentle caresses the trembling had abated and she had uncurled from her tight protective ball. In the course of reassuring Nell, Olsen and Lovell found that they had forgotten their own anger.

"Nell?" Lovell turned her tear-streaked face to face him. "Everything is okay now. *Reckon?"*

Nell nodded. *"Reckon."*

"Do you want to go back to your house?"

"Uh-huh."

"I'll take her back," Lovell whispered to Olsen. "Okay?"

"Go ahead."

Hand in hand, Nell and Jerry walked back to the cabin. Lovell felt ashamed that Nell had seen him—had seen both of them—so completely out of control and felt incapable of explaining anger like that.

When he was a child he had caught his own parents fighting like that, awakening in the night to the enraged voices of his mother and father. As far as Lovell knew his parents had been a happy couple with a stable marriage, but even they had the occasional knockdown, drag-out arguments.

The tensions and stresses that exist in any family would, once in a while, build to the breaking point and erupt in blind and angry discord. He had no clear recollection of what the arguments had been about— probably the same mundane subjects that afflict every marriage: money, pressures of job, sex and home, family; the grating unpleasantries of life. A jab, a cutting remark, then a spark that could erupt into an inferno of angry words and pain.

Lovell remembered how he would huddle in his bed listening as the argument built like a storm. He would lie in agony, tortured by his fears, afraid that his parents didn't love each other anymore and that the family would be torn apart by their animosity; and worst of all that somehow all this naked enmity was his fault, that he had brought it into being.

Lovell would cover his ears and rock his head from side to side, singing to himself, listening to his own voice filling his head. He would do anything to shut out the sound of anger.

And then it would be over.

It never failed to amaze him that by morning the storm would have blown over, that life continued on as it always had. Lovell would watch his parents over breakfast, observe them doing the things they normally did, as though nothing untoward had happened. He could never quite believe that they had forgiven each other, that they wouldn't remember each hateful thing said and nurse a deep and abiding grudge, a secret loathing.

As he grew older he learned of the remarkable restorative properties of the human body and spirit, that bruises fade and that hard feelings can scab over and vanish like old wounds. But somehow he didn't really trust the process. In his own marriage he had been so afraid of confrontation that he had never fought with his wife. Not even when she said she was leaving him.

Lovell left Nell at the door of the cabin and then started back toward the houseboat. Halfway along the track he noticed that Olsen was down at the jetty, at the very end, staring up into the star-dappled sky. He approached her shyly, the nasty things he had said to her still fresh in his mind. He felt ashamed of himself.

"She okay?" she asked.

"Yes."

"Sorry about that . . ." She gestured toward the houseboat, as if the wreckage of their anger and their argument was still strewn about inside.

"Me too."

"My mom and dad used to go at it like that," said Olsen, smiling. "Very loud. Very dramatic."

"I was just thinking the same thing. About my parents," he said. "Seemed like the end of the world."

Olsen nodded. "And when my mother said that I shouldn't worry, that moms and dads fought like that sometimes . . . I didn't believe her."

"Me neither."

They were silent for a moment, listening to the music of the wind on the water.

"My mother used to say that it cleared the air," said Lovell. "That a good fight got things out in the open. Do you think that's true?"

"I don't know," said Olsen slowly. "It's been a long time since I had a fight like that."

"I guess this situation is kind of claustrophobic. I mean, we're rivals, but we're working side by side."

"I guess." Paula glanced toward the cabin. "What do you suppose Nell made of it?"

Lovell laughed. "Her reaction was exactly the same as mine. I was a ten-year-old kid and I just wanted it to stop. I didn't care where it had come from, who was right and who was wrong—I just wanted it to be over. That's all Nell wanted too."

"I guess."

"Listen," he said. "Whatever I said back there—I was just sounding off. What do I know? I don't know anything about you. Pay no attention."

"You know enough," said Paula. "You know enough to zing me a couple of times."

"Yeah? Well, you didn't pull your punches either. I feel like you cracked a couple of my ribs."

"Hell," said Olsen, laughing. "*You* were going to smack me with a frying pan."

"Now, come on. You didn't think I was really going to do that, did you?"

"You looked pretty pissed off."

"You had hit a nerve. Pretty good aim. How did you manage that?"

"I guess we've told each other more than we realized these last few weeks."

Lovell rubbed his face and laughed out loud. "I don't recall telling you I was a blob."

"I worked that out for myself."

"Amazing. Took my ex-wife two years to figure it out. Course, she wasn't a professional mind reader like you."

Olsen grinned, disarmed by his out-and-out honesty. She was silent a moment, thinking that one confidence required another in return. "I have been reporting back to Al Paley."

Lovell nodded. "I know that. And you're right . . ."

"I *am*?" She sounded genuinely surprised.

Lovell grinned. "Bet you never thought you'd hear me say that, did you? Are you impressed by my magnanimity?"

"Depends. What am I right about?"

"That we have to have a plan for Nell. I just don't want her shut away in some hospital, that's all. I truly believe that if she is taken away from here she'll die."

"You may be right about that. And I certainly don't want her in a hospital."

"You don't?"

"Hospitals are for people who are ill," she said. "People who cannot take care of themselves. If Nell can handle her own life, then she has no business being in a hospital."

"That's a big if," he said soberly. He looked around the clearing. "She can live here as long as someone provides her with enough to eat. But if you think she has to interact with the outside world . . . That's a different story altogether."

"There's only one way to find out," said Olsen.

"And what's that?"

"Take her out and see how she does . . ."

TWENTY-ONE

Nell gazed with fascination at her own reflection in the tall mirror, but this time she was not looking beyond her image and into the eyes of her dead twin and the world they shared beyond the looking glass. This time she was looking at herself—herself alone—and was scarce able to believe her eyes. Nell was no longer wearing her washed-out, loose-fitting gray shift. Instead, she had put on a simple, navy-blue cotton sundress, one of Paula Olsen's, but the effect was dramatic. The dark color of the material highlighted the delicate white of her skin and the deep blue of her eyes. A stranger, unaware of Nell's true condition, would have perceived Nell to be a rather pretty young woman, casually but stylishly dressed.

Paula Olsen, standing behind Nell, watched in the mirror as Nell rubbed the cloth between her thumb and index finger, stroking the cotton gently as if it were some rare and fine material. Nell looked delighted at her new appearance and it was all Olsen could do to conceal her own smile. It was like watching a little girl playing dress-up in her mother's clothes. Nell was, for the first time in her life, in the throes of a naive and innocent vanity.

"Here," said Paula. "Let's add a little something to your new look. Try this." She held up a loose-fitting, long-sleeved beige jacket woven from a rough linen. She slipped it over Nell's slim shoulders and then took a couple of steps back to admire her handiwork.

"Looks good, doesn't it?"

Nell examined herself in the mirror, smiling broadly, enthralled by her new clothes, amazed to find that *she* was the person in the mirror. Her hands were busy exploring the pockets. She hauled a crumpled much-laundered dollar bill out of one of the pockets and unfolded it, her face darkening as she looked at it. She stared at the picture of George Washington with distrust.

"Eva'dur," she said primly.

"No, no," said Olsen. "He walks with the Lord."

Nell nodded, accepting the correction without question. *"An Mi'i. An' Maw."*

"That's right." Olsen made a mental note to make a written note about Nell's inability for critical thought. She would accept any information as certain truth and she would accept it from any source. It was a dangerous weakness, leaving Nell defenseless against outsiders who might have fewer scruples than did Olsen and Lovell.

"Okay, Nell," she said. "We aren't done yet." Paula pulled a comb and hairbrush from her purse and gathered Nell's short hair in her hands.

"This is a comb."

"Co'," said Nell.

"You use it on your hair." Olsen passed the comb through Nell's hair, surprised that it wasn't a snarl of knots and tangles. She made a part, then picked up the hairbrush and began brushing vigorously.

"Brush."

"Brush," Nell repeated dutifully.

She watched the whole process in the mirror, at first looking a bit mystified, but as her hair became soft and silky, Olsen could see that it was making sense to her.

"You look beautiful, Nell. Let's go show Jerry."

Lovell was waiting outside, sitting on the porch steps, but he jumped to his feet when Olsen and Nell came out of the cabin. His jaw dropped when he saw her, plainly astounded by the transformation.

"Wow!"

Nell hopped down the steps, grinning with pure pleasure. *"Jus' li' Pau'a,"* she said. As if to emphasize the point, she pulled up the hem of her dress, holding the fabric out to one side, and twirled like a dancer at a grand ball.

Lovell nodded. *"Just* like Paula. You look terrific, Nell. Really terrific."

"So are we going to do this?"

"I guess . . . If you think it's a good idea."

"I do. We'll take my car."

"Nell," said Lovell. "How would you like to take a ride in Paula's car?"

She looked at him, her eyes blank and uncomprehending—it was plain that she did not have the slightest idea what he was talking about.

Jerry shot a worried glance at Olsen. "Are you sure this is a good idea? The dress, the jacket, the hair . . . You don't think that's enough for one day?" He grinned. "Or am I being a blob again?"

"You're being a blob."

"Okay. You're the boss."

Jerry and Paula walked Nell across the clearing and showed her the low, sleek, bright red MG. Lovell opened the door and motioned toward the backseat.

"There you go, Nell. Get in."

Nell did not move.

"Show her."

"Okay." Lovell squeezed into the tiny car and dropped down onto the narrow seat. He patted the place next to him. "Come on, Nell. Right here."

Nell did as she was told. She had a curious little smile on her face as she stepped into the car, as if not quite able to believe what was happening to her.

Jerry Lovell thought that nothing Nell did could amaze him anymore—he was sure he had seen it all. But the full weight of her lack of experience of the workaday world struck him hard. Something as simple as getting into an automobile was an event that she felt intensely.

Olsen slipped in behind the wheel. "Everybody ready?"

"Let's go," said Lovell.

Nell jumped when the engine roared into life and she glanced nervously at Lovell.

"It's okay," he said, giving her shoulder a reassuring squeeze. "Don't worry about a thing."

When the car began to move, a look of such pure astonishment crossed Nell's face that Olsen almost laughed out loud. As the car began to jolt along the track, Nell swiveled her head to look back at the cabin, watching it grow smaller, plainly amazed to be moving away from it.

Next Nell turned her attention to Paula and her driving. Everything was fascinating—the turning of the steering wheel, the movement of Paula's hand on the gearshift, the creeping needles of the speedometer and rev counter—she took her eyes off these things long enough to flash Lovell a happy smile.

When the MG nosed its way off the forest track and onto the highway, Nell gazed in awe at the long ribbon of blacktop. Then there was a blast of an air horn and with a powerful roar a huge eighteen-wheeler truck came hurtling down the road, zooming past them. As the shock waves from the heavy vehicle hit, the light sports car rocked on its springs. Nell threw herself into Lovell's lap, whimpering in terror. She buried her face in his shoulder, hiding her eyes from the noisy behemoth.

"It's okay," said Lovell, taking care to keep his voice low and calm. "It won't hurt you. Don't worry. *Nay tata*, Nell."

Nell's curiosity overcame her fear. She sat up again, but clung to Lovell's arm. She grabbed him tight as a couple of cars streaked by, her nails digging into his skin.

Paula looked over her shoulder. "Okay? All set?"

Lovell shot her the thumbs-up. "Hit it."

She shifted into first and stamped on the gas. The car bucked, the rear wheels spun on the gravel road digging for traction, then they took off.

In the forest they had never traveled at speeds greater than fifteen miles per hour, but now, in a matter of seconds they were traveling at fifty.

Nell squeaked in alarm and hid her face in Lovell's shoulder—but again her inquisitiveness got the better of her. She risked a single quick peep and glimpsed the blur of trees at the side of the road. The sight was too unnerving and she hid her eyes again—but not for long. This new world was far too exciting, far too interesting. In spite of her fear she was forced to look.

"How's she doing?" Olsen yelled into the wind.

"Pretty good. She's getting the hang of it. She'll like it eventually. I think."

As if to prove him right, Nell pulled away from him, head up now, her eyes wide. She was trembling slightly, but not in fear—Nell was beginning to experience the pure excitement of high speed.

The wind was racing through her hair. Suddenly she thrust her arms into the air, her hands planing in the wind.

189

Then she started to yell, a loud, joyous holler, expressing her pure thrill at going so fast.

"Aah-aaa-yaa-aaa! YAAA—WAAA—WOOOOOO!" It was a loud, ecstatic sound. Pure happiness—Nell couldn't have begun to put into words, in any language, what she was feeling at that moment, but Lovell understood her perfectly. It was exactly the sound he had always wanted to make when *he* raced down the highway in a convertible sports car.

Impulsively he joined in Nell's pure celebration of speed. He waved his hands in the air and joyfully screamed at the top of his lungs. *"Wooo-eee-wooo-eee!"*

Paula Olsen could see both of her passengers framed in her rearview mirror. Nell was in a delirium of delight, her hair whipped by the rushing air, howling at the top of her voice. Paula Olsen had driven this road a hundred times in the past weeks, but never before had it seemed like a magical, vibrant thing to do. Nell's unvarnished enthusiasm was infectious. Suddenly Paula was screaming too.

"Yow-eee! Yow-eee-yow-eee!"

They screamed all the way into town, the car racing through the outskirts of Richfield. They screamed by gas stations and trailer homes, past a few shops and road-houses, the junkyards and strip malls that made up the outskirts of any small town.

Nell stopped screaming when a phalanx of loud motorcycles pulled up behind them, then with the hot roar of powerful machinery they blasted by—Billy Fisher leading the pack. The other bad boys of Richfield—Jed, Shane, and Stevie—were fanned out behind him, like a flying wedge, filling both lanes of the road. Nell could only gape.

The MG flashed by Lorene and Calvin Hannick sitting in their armchairs outside of their tumbledown trailer. The couple stared blankly, registering nothing, as the sports car zoomed by.

Nell found even the Hannicks fascinating, craning her head to watch as the stolid couple disappeared behind them. Lovell realized that even people as boring as the Hannicks would fascinate Nell—beyond her mother, himself, Olsen, and a few others, Nell had seen no human beings in her entire life. Every single one she encountered would be unique, rare, and singular before her astounded eyes.

Things that Lovell had ceased to see long ago were wonders to Nell—like the Jolly Chef Diner, a broken-down greasy spoon of a restaurant on the edge of Richfield. The food there was unexceptional, the service surly, and the hygiene suspect, yet to Nell it looked like a place of miracles. The most remarkable feature of the diner was the plaster statue of the Jolly Chef himself who adorned the ramshackle roof of the restaurant. The figure had an idiotic grin painted on its cartoon face. Nell saw it and grinned back, perfectly mimicking the expression.

Paula slowed the car as they entered the town proper. "Welcome to Richfield, Nell."

Lovell found it astounding that Nell could have lived for so long so close to the town and yet never had any idea that the place existed. Of course, for a person who had lived in such complete isolation, the very concept of communal living, of having neighbors or a neighborhood, of casual communication with strangers, would be almost impossible to understand. There was so much she had to learn.

Paula Olsen pulled the car into a parking space on Main Street, easing the MG into a slot right next to Sheriff Petersen's squad car. Nell stared at the few pedestrians passing by on the sidewalk and she was flabbergasted by the sheer number of people there were in the world. No one was paying the slightest attention to Nell—no one except a little boy of six or seven who was toddling down the sidewalk behind his mother. He alone noticed her odd, intense stare and he gawked back at her for a moment. Then he pulled his face into a grimace and stuck out his tongue at her. Nell did exactly the same thing, imitating him perfectly. Shocked that an adult would do such a thing, the little boy dissolved in tears and clutched at the hem of his mother's dress. Nell looked downcast, dismayed that she had inflicted pain on a child.

Jerry Lovell got out of the car and held the door open for her. "Okay, Nell. This is it." He took her hand and guided her to the sidewalk. "This is the excitement you've been missing all your life." He surveyed the sleepy main street of the town, looking from one end to the other. "I don't know about you, but I feel faint already."

"Hey, Lovell. How's it going?" Jerry turned and saw Todd and Mary Petersen coming out of the police station making for their car.

"Hey, Todd. Morning, Mary." Mary Petersen did not respond to his greeting. Lovell could see that the sheriff's wife was in better shape now than the last time he had encountered her, but she still had that blank, lifeless look on her face, as if she was only marginally aware of where she was or who she was with.

"Ms. Olsen," said Petersen. "You're still with us, I see."

"Very much so, Sheriff," said Paula.

Then, to his surprise, Petersen realized that the young woman standing there between Olsen and Lovell was none other than the mysterious Nell. "Well, I'll be . . ." he said. "How about this?"

"We're conducting a little experiment," said Lovell. "Nell, this is Sheriff Petersen."

"Welcome to Richfield, Nell."

Nell's eyes swept across Petersen's face and came to

rest on Mary. She studied her closely, searching her face as if trying to read some inner meaning on the woman's empty expression. Mary's lifeless eyes merely stared back.

Lovell took Petersen by the arm and half turned him away from the group.

"I'm sorry I haven't been around," he said quietly. "Kind of had my hands full out at the cabin."

Petersen nodded. "I understand . . ." He shot a side-long glance at his wife. "There hasn't been a lot going on."

"How is she?"

"Mary's pretty much the same, Jerry. She's been in a quiet phase right now."

Nell continued to examine Mary's face. Then she reached out and touched her cheek, lightly brushing her fingers along her skin. The instant Nell touched her, Mary's eyes grew wide in surprise and she inhaled sharply, as if an electric charge had run through her. It was a small movement and unseen by Lovell or Petersen. Paula Olsen saw it and watched as the women's gazes locked together.

"Come on, Mary," said Petersen. "Time to get going."

Mary Petersen got into the car, but her eyes remained fixed on Nell, as if she were incapable of tearing them away. The sheriff glanced at Nell too, not quite able to believe that this docile, well-groomed young woman was the same person they had discovered on the day Violet Kellty died.

"Doing good work there, Lovell."

"Early days yet, Todd." Jerry took Nell's arm and started to walk her down the sidewalk. Mary Petersen's eyes followed Nell all the way.

Larry's Supermarket in the middle of Main Street was a run-of-the-mill food market—unless you saw it through Nell's eyes. To her it was a treasure house of valuables, a riot of color and stimuli. Nell wandered the narrow aisles staring at the merchandise, scarcely believing that there could be such a place on the face of the earth.

A display of toilet paper brought her up short. She blinked at the tall ziggurats of brightly colored rolls, her eyes filled with the astonishing hues—rose pink, honeysuckle yellow, mint green.

Then a golden rack of bottles of vegetable oil seized her attention and she pressed her face close to the glistening liquids. Through the bottles she caught sight of a mountain of apples, each one gleaming like a ruby.

Olsen and Lovell followed Nell down the aisle as she looked from side to side examining the things on the shelves as if she were in an art gallery—Nell's hands half reaching out, but afraid to touch these wondrous things. A woman pushed by with a shopping cart, grabbed a mammoth pack of disposable diapers, and casually tossed it into her basket. Nell seized a package herself and studied the photograph of a fat, rosy-cheeked baby sucking his thumb. Nell slipped her own thumb into her mouth in a fair approximation of the picture.

Gently Olsen took the package of diapers away and put them back on the shelf. "Those you don't need," she said.

"Why not?" asked Lovell. "Everyone else is taking what they want. Why can't Nell?"

Olsen put her hands on her hips and looked at Lovell with a cool, critical eye. "So what's the deal here," she asked. "We're supposed to let her have anything she wants?"

"Why not?" He glanced over at Nell who was in rapt examination of a display of Wonder Bread.

"She doesn't know what any of this stuff is. How can she know what she wants."

194

"So? Get her a shopping cart and let her find out for herself."

"Fine," said Olsen. "But you pay for it."

"Deal."

Nell pushed her cart through the store for more than an hour choosing items at random. By the time she was finished she had filled her shopping cart with a pile of green peppers, aluminum foil, a half a dozen cans of dog food, a plastic colander, and a whole array of thick oven mitts.

"This is ridiculous," said Olsen as Lovell unloaded the cart at the cash register. Nell watched as each item was pushed through the scanner, jumping slightly every time the machine emitted each little electronic beep.

"What's ridiculous about it?"

Olsen grabbed one of the cans of dog food from the shopping cart. "She's got six cans of dog food here—and she doesn't have a dog."

"Who says it's dog food?"

"I do," said Olsen. "See? It says right here. Puppy Chow. To me that means dog food."

"Sure. To *you* this is a can of dog food. To Nell it's an animal picture that comes with a round metal stand. It's just a question of perception."

"Please . . ."

Nell waited by the front door of the shop, staring out into the street. Behind her the clerk was bagging up her purchases and Lovell was patting his pockets looking for his wallet. Then he stopped and grabbed something off the rack by the register. It was a big bag of candy bars, a cellophane sack stuffed with all manner of cheap and gaudily packaged sweets. He tossed it on the belt with the rest of the purchases.

"Uh-uh," said Olsen sternly. "I'm not getting her that." She grabbed the bag and threw it back on the rack.

"Why not?"

"She hasn't eaten junk like this yet and I'm not having her start now."

Lovell laughed and shook his head. He retrieved the candy and put it back with the rest of Nell's purchases. "Come on. Lighten up. You mean she's *never* going to be allowed to even taste a little candy bar?"

Olsen felt a little tremor of irritation. "This is how it always plays out. Dad gets to be the cool, easygoing one, while Mom is the heavy who won't let anyone have any fun."

The cashier had her hand on the candy, waiting to see who was going to win the debate before running it through the scanner. Behind Lovell a woman with a full shopping cart sighed and rolled her eyes.

"Mom? Dad?" said Lovell, bemused. "Look, it's just a bag of candy bars. Not heroin. Remember how she loved that caramel popcorn? Just think how she's going to love chocolate."

"It's still a drug," insisted Olsen. "It's poison. You want to addict her to sugar?"

"Please, Paula, don't be such a tough guy. Don't you remember eating candy as a kid?" Lovell got a faraway look in his eyes. "Saturday morning, tearing a wrapper off a Babe Ruth? That first explosion of total sweetness? Life doesn't get any better than that."

"Oh, really? Still got your own teeth?"

Lovell flashed her a big grin, pulling back his lips, baring his teeth at her. "Mostly."

"You want to make up your mind, folks?" asked the cashier. "Got people waiting in line."

But Olsen had lost interest in the subject. She glanced around the front of the supermarket. "Where's Nell?"

TWENTY-TWO

Nell had wandered out into the street, intending to wait there for Paula and Jerry. But then she heard the music. It was music unlike any she had heard before, far from the melancholy melodies of Patsy Cline and Roy Orbison. This new music was different—harsh, pulsing thrash rock and it came pouring out into the street through the open door of Frank's Bar.

Oblivious to the light traffic on Main Street, Nell crossed over, following the trail of the music as surely as she had tracked the sweet popcorn across the clearing.

Frank's Bar had just opened for business and the only drinkers in the place at that early hour were the bad boys. Billy Fisher and Stevie lounged at the bar, cold longnecks in their hands, watching as Shane and Jed racked the balls on the pool table for the first of an interminable series of games of eight ball.

Frank, the bartender, set up four beers and retreated to a corner of the bar, as if trying to put as much distance between himself and his four best, but most annoying patrons. He buried himself in that day's copy of the *Snohomish County Prospector* and hoped that the boys didn't cause any trouble.

The four had already had a small squabble, wrangling over whose turn it was to feed the jukebox, an argument that went round and round until Shane stuffed a buck into the machine. His selections were predictable— Aerosmith, Guns N' Roses, Bon Jovi, Metallica—but he was more interested in buying a few minutes relief from the quarrel than in the music.

Billy took a swig from his beer and looked around the barroom. "This all we're gonna do all day? Just sit here?"

Jed lined up the cue ball and fired it down the table. Balls in the triangle scattered across the stained green felt. "Got any better ideas?"

Billy, of course, did not. He merely grunted and poured more beer down his throat.

None of them had any work that morning; in fact, they had nothing to do all day, and they were already bored. They loved beer and they loved pool—but it wasn't enough to fill their days, not even with their low expectations of life.

Right then Billy Fisher was simply resigned to the tedium of his existence, but a couple of beers from now he would be feeling mean, ready for a little trouble.

Nell, of course, had no idea that she was entering in on such an unpleasant situation. All she was interested in doing was finding the source of the intoxicating music. She stood in the doorway, backlit by the bright sun outside, feeling the spell the music had cast on her. She was staring into the tavern, listening intently, completely unaware of the people in the dark room.

It took a while for Billy to notice Nell standing framed in the doorway; he did an enormous, almost theatrical double take. He gawked for a moment, then nudged Stevie hard in the ribs.

"Look," he whispered. "It's her. It's that wild woman I told you about."

Stevie looked over his shoulder, glancing at Nell. All he saw was a pretty young woman in a summer dress— admittedly a rare sight in Frank's at any time of the day or night—not the screaming harpy that Billy had told them about.

"She ain't wild," Stevie said. No one had ever accused Billy Fisher of being careful about the truth.

"I tell you," Billy insisted. "It's her. It's the god-damned wild woman."

"Like hell."

Billy ran an appreciative eye over Nell's body. The glaring light of day threw her into stark contrast against the gloom of the bar. The dazzling illumination made her dark dress translucent, the outline of her slim body visible under the thin material.

Billy took another swig of beer and wiped his mouth with the back of his hand. "Wild woman or not," he said, leering at her, "she's got nothing on under that dress."

Stevie's head whipped around and saw that, for once, Billy Fisher was telling the truth. "Whoa," said Stevie. "She ain't wearing no bra neither."

Nell was unaware of their interest. She had followed the music and realized that it came from the brightly lit box in the corner of the bar. Her eyes fixed on the jukebox, she edged into the room.

Billy winked at Stevie, then slipped off his bar stool, swaggering up to Nell. "Hi there, baby. So how you doin' today?"

Nell took her eyes off the jukebox and stared at him for a moment.

"How about I buy you a drink, honey?" said Billy, doing his best to be charming. "You wanna beer?"

Nell continued to stare at him. At the pool table, Jed tried to sink the number three ball in the side pocket, but

199

missed, sending three or four balls scurrying across the green felt. Nell heard the click of the balls and turned to watch them roll across the table.

Billy Fisher grinned and stage-whispered to Stevie. "She's a dummy," he said.

"Cute dummy," said Stevie.

"Best kind," said Billy, ogling Nell's breast. "Hey, honey, you don't understand a word I'm saying, do you?"

The billiard balls had stopped rolling and Nell turned her gaze back to Billy. She was only partially aware that Billy was even speaking to her. Her head was filled with the music and it rooted her to the spot.

"Hey, Jed, Shane," Billy called. "Get over here . . ."

Shane was bent over the table, his pool cue extended, lining up his shot. "What for?"

"Get a load of this."

The two pool players looked up and, for the first time, saw Nell.

Shane grinned, showing a mouthful of uneven teeth. "Hey, sugar," he said.

"Who's she?" asked Jed.

"Friend of mine." He winked broadly at his friends. "Watch this." He pulled up his T-shirt, revealing the tight muscles of his belly. "You like to see my body?" He rippled his muscles as seductively as he could. "Nice, huh. You like to show me yours now?"

Shane, Jed, and Stevie had moved a little closer. All three were grinning.

"Hell yes," said Stevie.

"Show 'em."

"You got nothing on under that dress, right?" Billy smiled and winked, pointing to the dress. "Like to take it off?"

Nell understood that he was talking about her new clothing and was proud that he had noticed that she was so nicely dressed. She pulled up the hem, just as she had on the porch steps of the cabin and turned slightly, as if modeling the garment.

Billy cackled and clapped his hands. "That's right, honey. You gonna show us what you got."

The others roared with laughter and howled, their boisterous howls almost drowning out Nell's words.

"Jus' li' Pau'a," she said.

"Yeah, whatever." Billy clapped his hand against his chest and grabbed his own breasts. "Show them pretty little titties, baby!" He turned around and waved his backside at her. "C'mon, honey, show that tight little ass!"

"Billy . . ." Frank cautioned. The bartender put down his newspaper and felt for the leather-covered lead weight he kept under the bar. He didn't want things to get out of hand but he would use the weapon if he had to. It would not be the first time he had introduced his club to the back of Billy Fisher's head. It was part of doing business in Frank's place.

"C'mon, Frank," said Billy hotly. "We're just having a little fun."

Nell had understood Billy's pantomime. She had no sense of modesty or shame and Jerry had convinced her that men were not the evildoers she had been led to believe they were.

Abruptly the music clicked off, Shane's dollar having played out. The moment of silence broke the spell of the music. In the sudden silence, Nell shook off her jacket, then reached down and grabbed the hem of her dress and hauled it over her head, tossing it to the floor. She stood there naked but for her panties and sandals.

Their laughter froze on their faces and one by one their jaws dropped open. Suddenly the boys felt nervous, out of their depth. Not even Billy had really believed that Nell would take off her clothes. Even Frank—who had more or less seen it all in the bar business—looked shocked.

Nell's clear eyes gazed at them and they couldn't take the directness of it, the focused simplicity and lack of guile. Nell was innocent and suddenly they all felt ashamed of what they had done. They backed away from her as if she were red-hot.

"Nell!" Lovell was standing in the doorway. He pounded into the barroom. "What the hell!" He scooped up Nell's clothing and tried to put it over her head. Lovell turned on the boys who were stepping back. "What the hell have you done to her?"

"Nothing," mumbled Billy. He wouldn't meet Lovell's angry eyes. "We ain't done nothing, Doc. She's just crazy, that's all. Crazy."

Nell listened to Billy and understood only one word. "Crazy?" she said. Then she started to sing. *"Crazy— Fo' thinkin' tha' ma love coo' ho' you—"*

"Oh, Nell . . ." said Lovell, suddenly very weary. He pulled the dress over her head and guided her arms into her sleeves, dressing her as he would a little girl. "What am I going to do with you?"

From within the folds of her dress, Nell continued to sing her song. *"Ah crazy fo' tryin' . . . An' ah—"* Her head popped out through, above the collar, her eyes shining at Lovell. *"Crazy."*

"Polymorphous perversity," said Olsen to Lovell. They were leading Nell down the sidewalk on Main Street. She was humming to herself, happy and completely unaware that anything untoward had taken place in Frank's bar.

"There was nothing perverse about it," said Lovell. "She had no idea what was going on."

"Well, yes and no. Polymorphous perversity is a high-falutin' psychological term for what boils down to

202

the old 'you show me yours, I'll show you mine.' It's a nasty name for perfectly normal infantile sexual behavior."

"All those games of doctor when I was a kid—that was polymorphous perversity?"

Olsen laughed. "More or less."

"It's no wonder I chose medicine as a career."

"Nell hasn't identified the genitals as a source of sexual activity yet," Paula explained. "Nor does she know anything about intercourse—but somewhere in the back of her mind she knows *something* is going on."

"Should we tell her?"

"Do you want to do it?"

"No. Do you?"

"*You're* the doctor."

"Yeah, but—" He seemed to squirm in embarrassment. "I'm not that good at this sort of thing."

"Then what are we going to do? Wait until she runs into Billy Fisher and his friends again?"

"They were scared to death," said Lovell. "They wouldn't dare lay a hand on her."

"Well, what if they had had a couple more beers? What if she runs into someone who *would* dare to lay a hand on her? You know as well as I that someone in diminished capacity is at risk for sexual abuse."

"She's *not* diminished," Lovell insisted.

Paula Olsen was in no mood to squabble over terminology. "Nell is vulnerable, Jerry. She should have some idea what sex is all about."

"Okay, okay . . . You take her back to the cabin. I'll take care of it . . ."

Jerry Olsen borrowed Amy Blanchard's car and a few minutes later was racing down the mountain to Monroe. It was the only town of any size in the area, the only town large enough to boast a real bookstore—literature-loving

203

Richfielders had to be content with a rack of paperbacks in the local drugstore.

Still, the book shop in Monroe was no great shakes and Lovell wasn't even sure that it would have what he was looking for.

"Do you have a section on sex education?" he asked the sales assistant behind the main cash register. He kept his voice low and as he spoke he glanced around the store, hoping he would not see anyone he knew. Lovell knew it was stupid, but he felt like an underage kid trying to buy a copy of *Playboy*.

The saleswoman smiled perkily. "We sure do. Would that be for an adult or child?"

Lovell was sure the woman had no idea how hard it was to answer a question like that. He hesitated a moment. "Child, I guess."

"Okay. Follow me." She walked through the store, Lovell trailing behind. "How old is the child?"

"Ah. Well . . . She can't read yet."

"So you'd want something with pictures, right?"

Lovell nodded. "That's right."

The saleswoman ran her eye along a shelf of books. She pulled one down and showed it to him. "Okay-ay," she said. "Here you go."

"*So Where Did I Come From, Anyway?*" Lovell read. "Now that's a question I guess everyone asks at one time or another. Right?"

The saleswoman was beginning to wonder if she didn't have a weirdo on her hands. "Uh-huh. They say that it's very popular with the parents."

Lovell flipped through the book. The print was large and simple, the drawings cartoonish and brightly colored. There were pictures of frolicking birds and buzzing bees, as well as Mommies and Daddies and little children, hugging and happy. There were even childish drawings of sperm cells and eggs—each with a big happy face.

"I don't see any pictures showing what actually . . . happens," said Lovell. "You know, a man and a woman actually engaged in—"

"Oh," said the saleswoman quickly. "You want *adult* sex education."

Lovell looked puzzled. "Aren't children supposed to know about it?"

The woman laughed nervously. "Well, it's a sensitive issue, isn't it? So many stories you hear these days. They're only young once, aren't they?"

"I suppose . . . Look, I'm sort of in a hurry and I was wondering if you had something a little more . . . something a little more graphic."

"For a child?" The saleswoman looked as if she was considering calling the police.

"No."

"You *did* say a child, sir."

"Yes. Yes, I know I did." Lovell swallowed hard and could feel himself begin to sweat. "But it's actually for me."

The saleswoman gave him a long, hard look—the kind of look that suggested that if he didn't know where babies came from by now then it was probably too late. "Of course."

From a high shelf on the other side of the store she retrieved a thick book. The cover art was a tasteful line drawing of a naked couple entwined in each other's arms.

"There you go, sir. *The Story of Love*."

Lovell took the book in his hands. The book was encased in a thick sheath of plastic wrap. "Am I allowed to open it?"

"Of course, sir," said the saleswoman. "Right after you've bought it . . ."

Jerry Lovell made it back to the cabin before the sun went down. Nell had changed out of Paula's clothes and back into her old shift and was sitting on the porch with Paula. Her face lit up when she saw Jerry.

"Je'y!"

"Hi, Nell. I've brought you a present." He placed the book in her hands, Nell accepting it reverently as if it were a sacred thing. This made perfect sense, of course. Up to that point in her life there had been only one book, her beloved family Bible, the Word of the Lord.

"Wor'i'a law?" Nell asked.

Lovell shook his head. "Not quite."

Nell looked curiously at the book, turning the pages, one after the other.

"Nell," said Lovell. "I want you to take a look at this book. We'll be waiting over there." He pointed to the canvas awning. "If you have any questions about any of this, then you come and ask us. Okay, *reckon?*"

Nell nodded, but did not take her eyes off the book. *"Reckon, Je'y."*

"Good."

Lovell and Olsen withdrew, settling under the sunshade. "I didn't want to stand over her while she went through the book. Thought it might make her self-conscious."

"She is not conscious of her self," said Olsen, gently taunting him with the idiom of her profession.

"Enough with the jargon. She'll be good and self-conscious when she gets a good look at the pictures in that book. Give her a good case of the guilts—just like the rest of us."

"The Story of Love?" Olsen laughed. "I want to borrow it after her because I can't wait to find out how *that* story comes out."

Lovell smiled sheepishly. "Sure, it's hokey. Maybe you have a better idea?"

"No," she said with a shrug. "*The Story of Love* will have to do, I guess."

They sat in silence for a while, watching Nell across the clearing. She was deeply absorbed in the book, her attention concentrated on every detail of every picture. Both Lovell and Olsen found it funny as well as touching to watch her, the range of expressions changing every moment on her mobile features. She turned the pages, her emotions running through incredulity, shock, and awe; she caught sight of something and her delighted laughter rang out in the evening air.

"Someone laughs at me like that and I'll be celibate for the rest of my life," said Lovell.

"Don't take it so personally."

"You haven't realized by now that I take *everything* personally?" asked Lovell.

"Now that you mention it . . ."

Lovell cocked his chin in Nell's direction. "Did your parents do this for you? Get you a book that spelled out the whole mystery of sex?"

"You must be joking. My mother would die before she gave me a book like that. Did *you* have a book?"

Lovell nodded. "Uh-huh. You bet. *The Youth's Guide to Life and Love.*"

"That would just about cover it."

"Hardly. It was so obscure it made as much sense to me as Nietzsche would have. I had a feeling it was sexy, but I couldn't put my finger on it. So to speak."

"Well," said Olsen, "I didn't even have that much."

"So how did you learn?"

"Girlfriends at school. You? How did you hear the facts of life?"

"My brother Jack told me. He was six years older than me. I thought he had all the answers. I mean, how could

I not? Jack had a *driver's license* already. You have to trust someone that Dad would trust with the Oldsmobile, right?"

"Really? How old were you when he told you?"

Lovell looked at the sky and then down at Olsen. "I must have been about ten years old. I had heard rumors about it already. Turned out that he just confirmed the hearsay. But he told me one thing I didn't know. It made a real impression on me."

"What? What was it?"

Lovell laughed, recalling the old memory. "Jack told me that when you make love to a woman—he didn't put it quite that delicately—Jack said, your body takes over."

"Takes over?"

"Yeah. He said it was like you're on autopilot. I never forgot that. But the first time I went with a girl—" He winced. "No autopilot. I waited. Nothing."

"That's pretty smooth, Slick," said Olsen. "You must have had women camping outside your door."

"Not exactly."

"So what happened?"

"Oh, God." Lovell could only laugh at himself. "After a while the girl said, 'I can't do it for you, Jerry.' I wanted to die. I was sure my first time would be my last."

"Autopilot! Jesus."

"I was young and stupid," said Lovell, anxious to defend himself. "And I had an idiot for an older brother. Like that's my fault."

Nell was coming toward them, crossing the clearing, *The Story of Love* in her hands. She stopped in front of Lovell and Olsen and showed them a two-page drawing of a man and woman making love. The illustration was restrained in the sense that it was not titillating or pornographic, but it left nothing to the imagination.

"Je'y?" asked Nell, she was turning to and fro, shyly like a little girl.

"Yes, Nell."

"How yo' caw this?" She pointed to the drawing.

"That's called making love, Nell."

"Makin' love . . ." She thought about this for a moment, then she mouthed the words silently, as if committing them to memory. Then she pointed to the man in the picture. *"Je'y."* Then she pointed to the woman. *"Pau'a."*

Jerry glanced at Paula and shifted uncomfortably. "Well, not exactly—"

Olsen cut in, nodding vigorously. "That's right, Nell. That's Jerry and Paula."

Nell seemed very pleased to hear this information. She put the book aside and took hold of Lovell's hand, making his fingers stroke Olsen's cheek. Then she took Olsen's hand and made her stroke Lovell's cheek.

Nell took her own hands away, sat back, and watched what she had put into motion. She whispered, "Makin' love."

Lovell's eyes were on Olsen as they touched each other, and he held his touch a moment longer than she held hers. He was surprised by the sudden warmth of his own desire . . .

That night, Nell lay in her bed thinking about the hundreds of wondrous things she had seen and heard that day. Her new clothes hung on a clothes hanger dangling from a nail in the wall. Nell looked at them, a tingle of happiness trilling within her, amazed and delighted that she had such a beautiful set of clothes.

Nell was still thrilled by her first encounter with speed—she could still feel the wind in her hair. She was amazed by the number of people she had seen, and still distressed by the sad woman she had met on the street.

She was astonished by the enormous quantity of strange and peculiar items in the grocery store; she was mystified by her encounter in the bar.

But it was the book that had most touched her. As she thought about what she saw her eyes filled with a faraway sadness. Deep inside her she could feel something, something like an ache, as she yearned for the closeness that she could sense coming off the pages of the book.

In the dark, Nell held out a hand, her fingers combing through the gloom as if searching for something. Then, magically, her fingers laced into another hand and Nell conjured up the image of her twin.

They whispered together. *"Chicka, chicka, chickabee . . . Thee'n me an' me'n thee . . . Ressa, ressa, ressa me . . . Chicka, chickabee . . ."* Suddenly Nell was seven years old again and still lying in her bed, the two sisters curled together in each other's arms, entwined like lovers.

TWENTY-THREE

Neither Lovell nor Olsen had realized just how trying and emotional the day had been until after dinner and a couple of glasses of wine. Jerry looked at Paula differently. He had woken up to her loveliness and it disturbed him. Olsen, for her part, was not oblivious to the subtle shift in their relations—not just between them, but between Nell as well.

"Do you think what we're doing is wrong?" Paula asked.

"What are we doing?" Lovell wasn't sure he wanted to hear her answer.

"We're allowing ourselves to become Nell's parent figures. Can that be good?"

"I guess it depends on what kind of parents we are. Wouldn't you say?"

"It can only help if . . ."

"If?"

"If we look like we're getting on. She can't see us fight like we did the other night. It's a deeply embedded instinct, wanting the authority figures in your life to form a secure bond."

"The fear of Mommy and Daddy fighting in the night, right?" Lovell poured himself another glass of wine.

"That's right. The pictures in the book meant a lot to her," Paula said. "That's why I let her identify us with those drawings. I hope you don't mind."

Lovell shook his head. "No."

"All the research shows that children who perceive their parents as having a good sex life grow up to make far better sexual relationships themselves."

"Is that so? Is that what the research shows?" Lovell couldn't help but smirk a little bit. "Is it that important that Nell have a good sex life—at this stage, at any rate."

"Can't hurt."

Lovell sipped his wine. "So did your parents have a good sex life?"

It was Olsen's turn to smirk. "Three guesses."

"Let me guess . . ." He studied her over his plastic cup of wine. "Your father left your mother when you were . . . fifteen, right?"

"Wrong. Eleven. All the research says that's the age kids take it the hardest." Olsen wasn't smiling now. Her eyes paled and a look of pain creased her face, as if her memory were pressing on a bruise.

"Why do you say it like that?"

"How am I supposed to say it?"

"Research," he said. "Always with the research. If it isn't in the research, then it didn't happen. Can't happen. Shouldn't happen. Is that it?"

"Research is what I'm about." She smiled faintly. "I've invested a lot of time in research. If the research is wrong, I've been wasting my time. Now *that* would be hard to face up to, at this stage."

Lovell shook his head. "No, that's not what you're

about. Far from it, in fact. I don't want to hear about the research. I want to hear about you."

"Maybe I don't want to talk about me."

"Why not?"

Paula shifted in her seat and looked away. She was always more comfortable being the one who asked the questions. "What is this? Some kind of interrogation?"

Lovell backed down immediately, throwing up his hands, as if defending himself. "Okay. Forget it. Sorry. I thought you'd be the kind who thinks it's good to get things out in the open. You know, talk things out."

"I don't go in for that," she said sourly. "I don't like that Oprah Winfrey school of therapy. You know, tell the world your secret shame, the audience claps, and you're cured by the final commercial."

"I'm not trying to heal you," Lovell protested. "Remember me? No drugs? No surgery. Me. Lovell. The fucking blob?"

"Oh. You." Paula managed a weak smile. "That's all right, then. I guess."

"But you know I *would* really like to hear about your secret shame."

"You know already."

"I do? Is it your gargantuan ears again?"

Olsen smiled and shook her head.

"Is it the man-woman thing?"

"Yup."

Lovell smiled broadly and raised his arms as if to embrace her. "How bad can that be? *Everybody* has some sort of secret shame about the man-woman thing. And from what I've heard the man-man thing, the woman-woman thing isn't any easier."

"Yeah? Well, my man-woman thing happens to be *my* problem. Let's just say I don't seem to have the trick of it." She sighed heavily and shook her head. "Don't you just hate life sometimes?"

213

"How do you know? You've hardly started."

"Oh, sure. I'm only twenty-nine." She was silent for a moment. "That's the same age as Nell." Paula was holding her wineglass, her forearm resting on the table. Abruptly her right hand began to shake, the tremor beginning in her fingers, then running all the way along her arm.

"Look at that, will you?" She held up her hand for his inspection. The quivering was pronounced. "It always does that when I get tense." She grabbed her right hand with her left in an ineffectual attempt to stop the tic. "Shit!" Paula jumped to her feet. Lovell could see that her eyes were moist, as if she was about to burst into tears. "Sorry. I'm going to have to take a walk."

Lovell was taken aback, not suspecting until that moment that their conversation was taking such an emotional toll on her.

"Is there anything I can do?" He looked genuinely distressed, pained that she hurt so much.

Paula Olsen did not trust herself to speak. She could only purse her lips and give a tiny shake of her head before walking down the gangplank and out into the clearing.

Far out, deep in the darkness, she stopped and doubled over. Her whole body was trembling now and she gasped for breath, trying to suck in as much of the cool night air as possible in the hope that it would calm her palpitating heart. Her talk with Lovell had churned her up inside and all kinds of long-suppressed passions and miseries came rolling up from somewhere beneath her soul. Warm, salty tears coursed down her cheeks and she buried her face in her hands, doing her best to stifle her sobs. She sank to the ground, her knees pressing into the soft soil, her hair hanging in her face.

Paula jumped when she felt a hand on her shoulder. "Dammit, Lovell," she snapped. "I said I didn't—"

"Pau'a?" Nell's eyes searched Paula's face looking for the source of her pain.

The shock and surprise of seeing Nell seemed to steady her somewhat. Olsen took a deep breath and tried to look calm. "Nell? Is anything the matter?"

"Anythin' a matter?"

Paula knew that Nell's words were nothing but blind mimicry, but it also sounded like a genuine question, as if Nell was really anxious to understand what was happening to her friend.

"Doana kee . . ." said Nell. It was the tone of voice one used to calm a child. She shook her head back and forth slowly as she spoke, *"Doana kee . . ."*

Olsen tried to shrug off Nell's concern. "I'm not crying," she insisted. But she couldn't control her tears. "Oh, hell. Yes I am." She brushed away her tears and tried to smile. "I'm supposed to be the one helping you."

Nell seemed to understand perfectly. She smiled knowingly, with a comprehension that Paula had never seen before. Then she put out one hand and stroked Olsen's cheek, her gentle, loving gesture. There was a simple care and concern there, a innocent tenderness that penetrated deep. She couldn't help herself. As Nell took her in her arms she began to cry, great wracking sobs that shook her body, a terrible wellspring of pain rising up inside of her.

Nell rocked her, caressing her hair, murmuring soft words, breathily, in Paula's ear. *"Doana kee, missa chicka. Doana kee, missa chickabee. Lilten, lilten . . ."*

Paula moaned softly and cried some more. She had no clear idea why she was weeping—it was nothing and it was everything. But she knew she needed to weep.

She cried for her past, for her parents' shattered marriage, for the father lost to her before she ever really had the chance to know him; for the family she had once had and lost.

She cried for all the sad, broken children she had seen, the ones she had studied so coolly, even as she fought with herself to stay remote, detached, and dispassionate. It was the same pattern that invaded her own interior life, this unwillingness to connect, her inability to make a bond, to work out what she had jokingly called the man-woman thing. Paula cried because she was afraid to fall in love.

She cried because she was tired. She didn't want to be strong anymore.

"Lilten pogies, lilten dogies," Nell whispered. Just as Paula had once had absolute faith in science and hard work, fieldwork and research, Nell sounded as if she had unconditional trust in the power of her soothing words. *"Lilten sees, lilten awes, lilten way, lilten alo'lay . . ."*

Her gentle hands followed her loving voice, soothing Paula into a calm silence. Nell bowed her head and drew Paula toward her. Paula let herself go and folded herself into Nell's embrace until their two brows were touching. They remained like this for a few moments, gathering stillness about them like a soft and comforting blanket. Their foreheads were pressed together, as if they were thinking in unison, their brains and bodies in synch as they communicated wordlessly.

Then Nell moved her face slightly and very softly rubbed her soft cheek against Paula's.

They knelt and nuzzled like animals, cheek against cheek, intimate and loving. Their eyes were closed, but Paula felt that she was seeing clearly for the first time in a long time. She saw that their roles had reversed—she was the one who had lost her way, the innocent who had gone astray in a bewildering and perplexing world. Nell was the guide, the pathfinder who would show the way out of the forest of confusion.

Nell was happy and relaxed. At long last she felt as if she had finally been reunited with her sister, her lost twin.

TWENTY-FOUR

The trees cast shadows, obscuring the calm blue-edge sunlight of morning in the clearing. There was no wind off the lake and the water was still, just barely lapping, scarcely disturbing the pebbles on the shore. Although it was early morning, both Lovell and Olsen were awake, the sounds of breakfast being made emanating from the galley of the houseboat.

Paula felt clearheaded and alert, the turmoil of the night before having been washed away, as if Nell had somehow made her pain vanish. She hadn't told Lovell about her encounter with Nell—she wasn't sure she ever would, fearful that Jerry would not believe her.

If Nell was awake, there was no sign of her within the cabin or in the surrounding woods.

Then Sheriff Todd Peterson's cruiser came crashing over the track in the forest, thoroughly destroying the morning calm that had settled on the clearing. As visitors to the clearing were unheard of—and unwelcome— Lovell came bounding out of the houseboat before Petersen's car came to a halt. He was relieved to see that their caller was friendly, but he was surprised to see that Petersen carried a passenger—his wife Mary.

"Todd," Lovell called out. "You've got Mary with you. Is everything okay?" He assumed the worst, that this was an emergency and that Petersen, unable to contact him to minister to his wife, had been forced to drive her all the way out here. Lovell had barely thought of his regular practice in the last few weeks. Now, however, he felt a prick of conscience and dismay—one day he was going to have to go back to the real world.

Petersen climbed out of his car, a newspaper folded and held under his arm. "Don't panic, Jerry. Nothing's wrong—at least, nothing's wrong with Mary. She wanted to come. Don't ask me why though . . ."

"Bring her in, Todd. Coffee's all made."

"Naww, it's okay. She wants to stay put in the car. She'll be okay." Mary did not appear to have heard any of this. She was staring fixedly across the clearing at Nell's cabin.

Todd Petersen held out the newspaper. "I'm sorry to have to tell you this, Jerry, but the story has gotten out."

Lovell felt his stomach lurch and something hard and tight spasmed in his chest. "Oh, Jesus," he sighed and his broad shoulders slumped. He looked at the story and was not surprised to see that it was written under Mike Ibarra's byline. The headline was everything he was afraid it would be—WILD WOMAN FOUND IN FOREST—and the subhead— *"Savage" Woman Is the Talk of Snohomish County* told curiosity seekers exactly where to look for her.

"Why couldn't they leave well enough alone, Todd?"

Petersen shook his head slowly. "Beats the hell out of me, Jerry. Maybe it makes people feel better to hear about someone they think is worse off. That's my guess."

Lovell plodded toward the houseboat. "You want to

have that cup of coffee, Todd? It comes with a floor show. Because when I show Paula this she's going to go ballistic."

Todd Petersen smiled. "Well, I guess so. It'll save you the trouble of calling the police."

But Lovell was wrong. Paula Olsen read the whole article through before saying anything and when she was done, she merely put the paper aside and shrugged.

"Well," she said, resigned to what had transpired. "It was always going to happen one day, I guess."

Lovell was so annoyed, so agitated by this unwanted publicity, that he failed to notice that Paula seemed changed from the night before—she was softer, calmer, more in control.

Lovell paced the small room, his anger radiating like heat. "What do we do? What the hell do we do?"

"Not much you can do," said Petersen.

"We continue as we started," said Paula. "And hope that people leave us alone."

"That's a really terrific idea," said Lovell sarcastically. "Got any more?"

"No," Paula said sweetly. "That's it."

"Dammit!"

"Maybe nothing will come of it," said Petersen. He was gazing out the window at the water.

"Like hell," said Lovell. "As soon as this gets out people will be coming up here, wanting to take a look at the freak who lives in the woods. They'll turn this place into a goddamn sideshow. It's not fair . . . It's not fair to Nell. She's not used to other people. And any outsiders are going to frighten her to death."

"The hospital, Jerry," said Paula. "Consider it, please. We can make sure she's safe there."

From outside they heard the sound of a car door slamming.

221

"Here they come now," said Lovell bitterly. "Vultures."

Todd Petersen was still at the window. "No. You're wrong, Jerry. It's Mary . . ." His wife had gotten out of the police car and was walking across the clearing, making straight for Nell's house.

"She's going into the cabin," said Petersen. He started toward the door, but Olsen stopped him.

"Let her go," she said.

"But she's going in there."

"I know. Let her go." She kept her voice low, but it was filled with a certainty and a quiet authority.

"Paula!" Lovell shouted. "What the hell do you think you're doing. Mary is a complete stranger to Nell. She might be harmless but Nell doesn't know that!"

"She isn't a complete stranger. They met yesterday, remember?"

"That doesn't mean a damn thing!"

"Yes it does." Neither man had seen the brief moment that had passed between Mary and Nell the day before. But Paula had witnessed it and after her experience with Nell the night before, she saw nothing strange in a troubled soul like Mary Petersen seeking solace with Nell.

"So what do we do now? Sell tickets?" Lovell looked out the window and saw Mary at the cabin door. Nell appeared and did not seem surprised to see her visitor. With a small smile she welcomed her in, then the two of them vanished into the dark interior of the house.

"What's going on?"

"Nothing sinister," said Paula. "Don't worry about it. Nell can take care of herself . . . Nell can probably take care of Mary too."

"We'll see about that." Lovell snapped on the video monitor. The image was clouded with static for a moment, then cleared. Mary and Nell were standing in the bedroom, their images reflected in the mirror. As Lovell settled down to watch, Olsen turned off the monitor and the screen went blank.

"What the hell are you doing now?" Lovell demanded.

"I think we should allow Nell and Mary some privacy."

"You don't want to see what happens?"

"Nope," she said calmly.

Lovell was incredulous. In the old days, Paula Olsen had spent hours in front of that monitor, observing Nell's most trivial movements, yet now, as she was about to interact with an almost total stranger, Paula was backing away.

"What about your precious research?"

Paula half smiled. "Research? I'm not all about research," she said. "At least, that's what *you* told me."

Petersen, still at the window, had been quiet through this exchange, more concerned about his wife than in Olsen and Lovell's professional squabbles.

"Well," he said finally. "You can argue all you want, folks—but it looks like you have a bigger problem right at the moment . . ."

Both Lovell and Olsen looked over at him. "What? What are you talking about."

Petersen nodded toward the window. "Looks like you've got your first sightseer."

Lovell threw himself at the window. Out over the lake, coming in low and fast, was a helicopter. One moment they could not hear it at all, and a second later the great roaring of the turbine engines seemed to well up out of nowhere. The machine hovered over the clearing, dark and threatening, the rotors kicking up a dust storm, the engines smashing the peace of the forest. The logo of a Seattle television station was stenciled on the tail and a cameraman aimed the blunt nose of a video camera out of one of the ports, filming the ground.

"Jesus! That thing is going to scare her to death!" Lovell raced off the boat and across the clearing, fighting his way through the wind created by the downdraft of the helicopter rotor blades.

He burst into the cabin—taken aback for a moment by the presence of Mary—and grabbed Nell, holding her, comforting her. Her thin body was trembling as if she were very cold. He could sense that she was on the verge of panic.

"It's okay, Nell. It's okay."

"Nell tata, Je'y." He could hardly hear her over the thunder of the helicopter engines.

Olsen and Petersen crashed into the room. "Mary," said Paula. "You okay?"

Mary Petersen flashed her a quick, timid smile. "I want to stay with Nell."

"Mary?" asked Todd. "What's going on?" He could see that there had been a change in his wife, that there seemed to be more of spark of life in her eyes.

"I came to see Nell," she said simply.

"We have to go," said Lovell. "Don't worry Nell, it won't be for long."

But the thought of leaving made Nell even more panic stricken. *"Nell tata, Je'y."*

"I know, I know," said Lovell, doing his best to sound reassuring. "But I'll be with you. I'll keep you safe. Jerry ga'inja."

Nell put her hand to him and he took it, his two big hands cradling her slim fingers. She looked deep into his eyes, the meaning unmistakeable: she was entrusting him with her life.

"Nay tata wi' Je'y," she said.

"Get us out of here Todd."

The four of them ran out of the cabin, Nell faltering for a moment on the threshold when the full weight of the

224

noise and confusion hit her, but Lovell urged her on, pulling her toward Paula's car.

Todd Petersen fired up his police cruiser and led the way out of the clearing. The helicopter backed off and circled, then zoomed back in over the clearing trying to follow the cars, but they had disappeared into the underbrush, the overhanging branches of the pines obscuring the track from the air.

But there were troubles on the ground too. A huge news truck came lumbering down the trail, filling the narrow road from shoulder to shoulder. Petersen did not flinch, aiming the police car straight at the behemoth, playing chicken. The truck emitted a blast of air horns, like the bellowing of an enraged bull and the driver yelled something but his nerve broke before Todd's. He wrenched the wheel violently to the left, driving the vehicle into the underbrush. Petersen swerved too, pushing the car up on to the verge—but he had opened the road like a line-backer, clearing a hole that Paula could slip her MG through. Olsen hit the gas and blew by the TV truck in a shower of dirt and gravel.

Mary Petersen watched the MG roar away and began to laugh. Her husband turned and stared at his wife and then began to laugh himself, a great release of tension and in sheer joy that his wife had been returned to him. He was stunned by the bright sparkle in her eyes, the animation in her features. He had seen that look before, when they were first together, when Mary had been the woman he had been so proud to marry. It was as if her smiling eyes were like sunshine, a risen sun, a signal that the long nightmare had come to an end.

TWENTY-FIVE

Nell's second trip out of the clearing was far less enjoyable than her first. She was nervous, made jittery by the unsettling events of the morning—Lovell could feel her next to him on the narrow car seat, trembling like a puppy. He put his arm around her shoulders and cradled her protectively.

"I'm here," he whispered. "It's okay. I'm here."

But Nell could not seem to gain control of her frazzled nerves and the further from home she traveled, the more high strung she became. She jumped every time a car passed them and as traffic intensified, the highway into Seattle became a collage of terrifying sights and sounds.

The torrent of heavy morning rush hour traffic flowing over the long swoops of the Evergreen Point Floating Bridge unnerved her. The Evergreen Point Bridge was the largest man made object she had ever encountered and it filled her with an almost overwhelming sense of panic. The arched lattice of steel seemed to flash before her eyes and the expanse of water surrounding was large, larger than the lake, an inland sea.

Lovell tugged at her hand. "Nell, look." He pointed toward the horizon as the skyline of Seattle appeared over the long rise of the bridge. The tall, three legged pinnacle of the Space Needle loomed through the urban haze. Nell blinked, not quite sure of what she was seeing. She turned a fear filled gaze on Jerry.

He had hoped that her natural curiosity might calm her, but he was wrong. The effects of her simple outing to Richfield had been dramatic and encouraging, but the sensory overload of the city was too much for her delicate system to bear. This new world was a place she did not know and did not want to know.

Nell's condition became more acute as they entered the heart of the city. They drove through the crowded streets, Nell staring with startled eyes at the traffic and the throngs of people crowding the sidewalks. Nell felt a stultifying claustrophobia enshroud her, as if the glistening plate glass windows of the office buildings were closing in on her. The noise assaulted her as well, the constant growl of car engines, the belligerent pounding of a jack hammer on a construction site, the frantic screech of sirens, the ceaseless roar of the city.

Nell burrowed into Lovell. "Okay, I've got you . . ." He glanced at Olsen. "She's not doing too good."

"It's not far . . . Hang on, Nell. You'll be fine, I promise."

But the hospital was just as scary as the world they had left behind outdoors. The bright lights of the emergency room seemed to sear Nell's brain, the masked people in surgical scrubs—were they men or women?—unsettled her, the drone of announcements from the public address system became a warped roar in her ears.

An orderly trundled by pushing a gurney. The comatose man lying beneath the sheets had the gray pallor of fatality, as if the only thing that stood between him and death, was the drip feeding into his arm. Nell shrank from the sight.

"It's nothing, Nell," said Paula. "Don't be afraid."

"It's a scary sight if you don't know what it is," said Lovell and held Nell closer.

Nell was beyond reassuring. She began to utter tiny cries, small, plaintive whimpers that Lovell knew presaged a panic attack.

"It's okay. You're safe here. I've got you."

Paula led them down a hallway and used a key card to open a locked door. The door slid open with a hiss. Nell cringed.

"This isn't going to work," said Lovell.

"Almost there. Hang on."

"She's going to blow."

Nell was whimpering louder now, swinging her head from side to side and tugging at Lovell's restraining arm. She was dragging her feet like a recalcitrant child, trying to slow their progress as if she knew that the deeper they went into the building the more danger they would be in.

"Carry her," Olsen ordered.

Lovell swept Nell up into his arms. "Here you go," he said. She put her arms around his neck and held him tight, a frightened little girl.

They were in the psychiatric wing now, the domain of Al Paley. Both Nell and Lovell felt the same thing—they were in enemy territory.

They passed the recreation room and Nell stared at the patients slumped in front of the blaring television, a crazy, frantic cartoon soundtrack filling the room. Through the distorted sound Nell heard someone . . . Someone calling her name.

She peered over Lovell's shoulder, frantically scanning the sad, slack faces for the source of the sound.

Then: there in a corner of the room was her twin, a tiny

229

blond girl in her patched smock and bare feet. She was huddled, almost doubled over as if against a biting cold. She called Nell's name plaintively.

In an instant, Nell had squirmed from Lovell's arms and dashed down the hall, unaware that she was running toward a hallucination. Suddenly Nell was hit by an individual thunderbolt, her body spread eagled in mid-air, her face smashed. She crumpled to the floor, leaving behind, suspended in space, a long smear of blood. Nell had pitched full speed into a plate glass window. Although half stunned by the impact, in a split second she was back on her feet, screaming like a wild animal, her body thrashing and contorting as she clawed at the glass.

"Nell! Nell! Please—" Lovell tried holding her in a bear hug, but she was in the throes of a terror fit, beyond hearing Jerry's voice, lost in her panic and fear. She was smashing herself against the glass, trying to break through.

"It's all right, Nell," said Lovell. "It's all right. I've got you—"

Paley emerged from his office and took in the scene. He snapped his fingers at two hefty male nurses. "Shelby! Carlo!"

"I can handle it," Lovell shouted.

"You want her to really hurt herself?"

The two orderlies smothered Nell, grabbing her in their beefy hands, pinning her arms to her side. The instant they touched her, she stopped struggling. She gazed at Lovell for a moment, blood and mucous smeared on her tear-streaked face. That look, the message in her eyes, cut into Lovell like a stiletto. Her eyes said: you have betrayed me. Then her eyes went blank, as if struck blind and her body slumped, limp and sagging in the arms of her captors like a animal playing dead.

When Nell awoke in her drab hospital room, Jerry Lovell was standing by her bed. Her eyes were open, but he could tell that her gaze was unseeing, unfocussed. Lovell spoke very softly.

"Nell? It's Jerry . . ."

There was no response, not even turning her head to look at him.

"Nell? Nay tata, Nell. Nay tata wi' Je'y."

Nothing . . . It was as if she was not living in her own body anymore, as if the soul had gone away. Lovell bit his lip, fighting back tears as he took her hand in his, cradling her hands the way she had shown him.

"Nell? Chickabee . . ." Lovell felt a great wave of despair wash over him.

"Nell! Don't do this! They'll shut you away! Show them how you really are. Please." He paused a moment, as if waiting for his words to sink in, but she did not respond. He dropped to his knees next to her bed and lowered his weary head onto the blanket. "Oh, Nell . . . Please . . . What the hell am I going to do?"

But Nell did not respond to his entreatries, staring into space, her mind and spirit far away from that place.

Paley brought his team of experts together later that day. He sat behind his large, imposing desk and looked at the grim faces of Malinowski and Goppel; Lovell was gray and defeated. When Nell gave up, he gave up as well. Only Olsen was still fighting.

"She hasn't freaked out like that for weeks, Al," she said. "You've seen the goddamn tapes. You know the kind of progress we've been making."

"I'm not happy about this, Paula."

"She's out of her familiar environment," she said. "You have to expect this."

"You've had almost three months. I am not happy. This kid needs help."

Lovell looked up, his face drawn with fatigue and full

of self blame. "I must have been out of my mind to bring her here."

Paley merely raised his eyebrows, but otherwise made no comment.

"She needs time, Al," said Olsen. "That's all. She'll calm down."

"Time?" said Paley. "Okay. We've got the weekend. Maybe by Monday I'll feel happier." He shrugged and stood up. "But maybe not . . ." He motioned toward the door. "I suggest we take a look at the patient."

Paley, Goppel, Malinowski and Lovell squeezed into the cramped confines of the observation room, their faces grey and indistinct in the faint light.

Paula was with Nell in the room beyond the glass, a Bible in her lap reading slowly. Her voice was thin and tinny in the observation room speaker.

"Whither is thy beloved gone, O though fairest among women? Whither is thy beloved turned aside, that we may seek him with thee." Paula paused a moment, glancing at Nell, hoping that her words had gotten through to her. "My beloved is gone down into his garden, to the beds of spices, to feed in the gardens, and to gather lillies . . ."

Lovell's eyes never left Nell's face, as if he could will her to respond.

"This isn't lower level autism," said Goppel. "That's for sure."

Paley nodded in agreement. "Hard to say what it is."

"I am my beloved and my beloved is mine," Olsen continued. "And he feedeth among the lillies . . . Though art beautiful, O my love, as Tizrah, comely as Jerusalem."

Lovell could see the pain in Nell's eyes and he raised his hand, as if he could touch her through the glass, but then he let it fall, knowing she was out of reach.

Lovell and Olsen walked Nell down the long hospital corridor, taking her back to her room. She remained as silent as unseeing as before.

"I want to take her out of here, Paula," Lovell whispered. "This place is killing her."

"Jerry, we can't. One more day, that's all."

Lovell shook his head. "You think the judge is going to say he knows better than Al Paley?

"Give me your car keys . . ."

"Jerry . . . Don't do something you might regret."

"I'm not. Far from it. Now give me your keys."

After a moment of internal tussle, she surrendered them. "I'm not sure that this—"

"I'm taking her out of here." Suddenly, he grabbed Nell and picked her up, sprinting for the door. The instant he touched her, Nell began screaming and kicking, her shrieks echoing in the halls.

"Jerry!"

Three nurses rounded the corner and stood between him and the door. Lovell barreled into them, hitting with all his weight, knocking them aside like nine-pins.

With Nell still kicking and screaming, Lovell burst out of the psychiatric wing making for Paula's car. He dumped Nell in the passenger seat, dove behind the wheel, fumbling to get the key in the ignition.

"C'mon, c'mon," he whispered. The engine turned over and he wrenched the machine into gcar. He floored the accelerator and the car fishtailed wildly as it roared out of the parking lot.

He drove aimlessly for an hour or two, all the while talking to Nell, trying to talk her back to natural state. She sat immobile in her seat, unfeeling, not hearing.

Twice he turned for home, starting the long climb up into the mountains for Richfield and twice he turned back. The clearing was probably over-run with sightseers now, TV crews were waiting, cameras ready, wanting their piece of the wild woman.

There was no place to go, no place safe. In desperation, he pulled the car off the road, driving into the forecourt of a motel out on Route 77. Nell allowed him to lead her into a room, a bedroom hardly more cheerful than the one she had left behind in the hospital. She sat by the window and looked out at the motel swimming pool, the highway beyond, and the red lump of the setting sun. She said nothing and did not look at him.

Lovell called Paula. "She hasn't said a word," he said. "Nothing. It's like she's died . . ."

"Where are you?"

"In a motel." He grabbed a book of matches off the dresser and read off the address. "Seventy-seven north, Huntersville exit. Room 209. You can see it from the road . . ."

"Stay put until I get there."

Lovell almost smiled. "Don't worry . . . We're not going any place."

Jerry hung up and looked at Nell. "Paula is coming," he said, hoping that even that small piece of news would get through to her.

"Nell . . . I never meant it to be like this. I'm not an angel," he said. "Just a man . . . Sorry, okay."

He waited for a response, but none came. *"Je'y feliss inna t'ee wi' Nell."* He shrugged. "But I guess all that's over now."

Nell's gaze settled on the swimming pool with its thick carpet of dead leaves floating on the surface. Before her eyes the undulating leaves changed and became a mat of leaves on the floor of her forest, then Nell could see the cave where she had hidden the bones of her twin. But she was there, alive, in her white smock dress, a garland of daisies woven around her neck.

She stood very still, Nell and her twin locked in a gaze. The little girl turned and walked away, moving away through the forest, breaking into a trot, then a run. She ran swiftly down the forest path, never losing her foothold, the forest a blur of green around her.

The little girl burst into the clearing, into a blaze of golden light. She slowed and walked along the bank of the lake, then stopped at the very edge of the water, the waves lapping at her bare feet. The child's eyes had grown grave and she raised her hands, palms outward, saying goodbye.

She stepped farther into the water, turning and letting her hands fall as she walked out into the depths. The water reached her knees, then her waist, then rose high enough to float the garland around her neck. Another step and the water closed with scarcely a ripple over her head, her blonde hair rolling for a moment in the water and then vanishing. All that was left was the ring of flowers floating in a pool of reflected light.

In Nell's mind, she spoke her own words of farewell. *"I am ma' belov'uh an' ma belov'uh is mine. She feede' amo' a lilies. Thou ah beau'fu, o ma love, a'Tizrah, come'ey a Jerus'em."*

She did not look at Jerry when she turned from the windows. She merely lay down on the bed, closed her eyes and went to sleep.

Nell had been sleeping for an hour when Paula finally made it to the motel. Lovell met her at the door, looking shamefaced and despairing.

Paula looked around the dreary little room. "Why here, Jerry? Why did you come here?"

"I didn't know where to go."

She looked at Nell then back at Lovell. "You know you're out of your mind?"

"Yes."

"So what happens now?"

Lovell sighed heavily. "I'm going to have to take her to court, aren't I?"

"Yes."

Lovell's shoulders slumped. "So that's it . . . Shit." Paula could see that he wanted to cry at the failure and frustration of it all. "I could take it if she'd say something to me. Anything but this silence . . ."

Olsen reached up and stroked Lovell's cheek. It was Nell's love gesture and she held his face and caressed him. His eyes shone with tears.

"Doana kee, missa chickabee."

She drew his face to hers and rubbed her cheek against his, slowly and tenderly, the way Nell did it. Paula took him in her arms and nuzzled against him, slow, gentle and intimately. In answer, he raised his finger to her cheek and stroked her, using Nell's special loving gesture. They looked into each other's eyes, each looking at the others thoughts. They didn't seem to need words to communicate now.

Then he kissed her on the mouth, the softness of his lips grazing hers. A natural reserve made her hold back for a moment, then she could feel herself letting go and kissed back, her mouth opening to him.

The kiss unleashed the passion that was buried deep within both of them and they held each other tight, tight, and kissed as if the was no one other place on earth and no other people but the two of them. It was like coming home.

TWENTY-SIX

Judge Hazan gaveled the proceedings into session at precisely nine o'clock on the morning of the day exactly ninety days from the last session.

It was a much different courtroom he presided over now, however. The gallery was packed with spectators and media from a dozen different outlets. There was a large contingent from Richfield—Todd and Mary Petersen, Amy Blanchard and Frank of Frank's Bar; sitting at the very back, all of them hoping that the judge would not see them, were the wild boys: Billy Fisher, Shane, Jed, and Stevie. They were relieved that for once they were in court and not sitting sullenly at the defendant's table.

"Who is appearing for the hospital?" the judge asked.

A man in a perfectly cut suit stood. "I am, Your Honor. Richard Weiss . . ."

Judge Hazan smiled. He knew the lawyer's name and his reputation—Weiss was one of the best trial lawyers in the state and his hiring suggested that the hospital was really playing hardball on this case. "I'm impressed, Mr. Weiss, that a man of your stature would make the trip all the way up here to our little court."

"The honor is mine, Judge."

Lovell leaned over and whispered in Don Fontana's ear. "Oh, shit. They're giving valentines to each other. That's bad, isn't it?"

"No," Fontana whispered back. "That's good for us. I guess that the hospital doesn't know that Hazan hates high-priced hired guns."

"Mr. Weiss, would you like to begin?"

"Yes, Your Honor . . ." Weiss rose and walked the length of the courtroom. He stopped in front of the table where Fontana, Lovell, Nell, and Olsen sat, flashing them a small smile before turning to face the judge.

"Your Honor, Nell Kellty is on the threshold of the most exciting journey any of us will ever make. The journey from the safe but narrow haven of childhood to the open horizons of maturity . . ." He paused for a moment, his eyes sweeping around the courtroom. "But to make that journey safely and successfully, Nell needs a guide . . ."

Judge Hazan was listening to Weiss, but his eyes were on Nell. It was plain that she fascinated him.

Richard Weiss pointed to Professor Paley. "This man, Your Honor, Professor Alexander Paley, has the expertise to help Nell. He has the financial backing of the National Institute of Mental Health. He has the facilities. He has the staff. Who better to guide Nell on her journey?" He swung around and looked at Jerry, the slightest tinge of contempt in his gaze.

"Dr. Lovell seems to think he can do a better job, yet he is a general physician with no training in mental health. Once upon a time he was a cancer specialist but his career came to a sudden end in unexplained circumstances . . ."

238

Weiss did not notice that Fontana was smiling slightly, trying to conceal the fact that Weiss had stepped directly into a trap.

"In addition, Your Honor, Dr. Lovell is a man who has damaged private hospital property, not to mention assaulting a senior staff member. Can a man like this provide and care for Nell at this crucial time? I think not . . ."

Fontana rose to his feet. "Objection, Your Honor. Dr. Lovell has no wish to act as Nell's keeper. Either now or at any time in the future."

A gasp like a breeze ran through the courtroom. Paley looked at Weiss who stared at Lovell.

Even Judge Hazan looked startled. "Then why are we all here?" he asked.

"To decide what's best for Nell, Your Honor," said Fontana simply.

Hazan leaned forward and peered over his glasses. "Am I to understand that Dr. Lovell is no longer offering his services in this matter?"

"That is correct, Your Honor."

Weiss had recovered from the surprise. "In that case, Your Honor, I move that custody be granted immediately. There are no other applicants here and it is agreed by all parties that Nell does need help. So—"

Lovell was on his feet. "That's not true, Your Honor. She doesn't need help. She doesn't need me. She doesn't need any of us. All you have to do is ask her."

"Ask her?" said Weiss. "Your Honor—"

Judge Hazan held up his hand for silence. "Hold on here. Mr. Fontana, what are you up to?"

"Nothing. Except we propose that Nell speak for herself, that's all."

Judge Hazan looked puzzled, but intrigued. He glanced at Nell. She sat composed and calm, as if she was following the proceedings without difficulty.

"Speak for herself?" said Hazan. "As I understand it there is some kind of communications problem, isn't there?"

"I can interpret, Your Honor."

"Dr. Lovell is an interested party," Weiss protested. "I don't think that he should—"

The judge's eyes twinkled. "Oh, I don't know about that, Mr. Weiss. He just said that he has withdrawn his interest in this case. If the young lady can speak for herself, so much the better. Let's see how it goes, shall we. Mr. Fontana, please put your client on the stand."

"Very good, Your Honor." Fontana took Nell by the hand and led her across the courtroom, seating her in the witness chair. Jerry took up his position beside her, but keeping a little back, showing Nell front and center.

Everyone in the courtroom had been waiting to get a proper look at her and a silence fell as they stared. Nell faced them, but now she looked small, frail, and nervous. She glanced at Lovell and got a quick smile of reassurance and support.

"Nell," said Don Fontana, "since your mother died you've been alone—"

Lovell translated as unobtrusively as he could, keeping his voice low and even. *"Fro'tye maw waw wi'a law . . ."*

Nell shook her head slowly from side to side. *"Nay. Je'y done come. An' Pau'a."*

"Jerry and Paula can't stay with you forever," said Fontana.

"Doan ress aw tye," Lovell translated.

Nell nodded again, not at all troubled by this. *"No'so ress aw tye,"* she said. *"Alo'so done come lone inna'tye erna feliss."*

"No one stays forever," said Lovell. "Everyone ends up alone in the big night."

Fontana nodded. "And aren't you afraid to live alone in the forest?"

"Nay tata inna kine?"

Nell thought for a moment before replying. *"Alo'so tata,"* she said earnestly. *"Alo'lay. Kine'ey law lilten, lilten us'kee, us'erna kee."*

"Everyone is frightened," said Lovell. "Everywhere. The sweet Lord soothes our tears, our many tears."

The room was completely still. Nell's presence and her words were mesmerizing the audience.

"Nell, do you want to leave your home in the forest and be looked after by this gentleman?" Fontana pointed to Professor Paley. Weiss jumped to his feet.

"Your Honor, I have to object to this. Nell knows nothing about Professor Paley or anything he has to offer her."

"Sit down, Mr. Weiss," said Hazan. "You'll have the chance to tell her. Dr. Lovell, if you would translate the question . . ."

"Nell wanna lea'a kine and ress wi'— " He pointed to Paley. Nell looked, studying him, Paley shifting anxiously under her long unnerving gaze.

When her answer came it was soft but unequivocal. *"Nay,"* she said.

"No more questions, Your Honor." Fontana sat down and gathered his papers.

Judge Hazan nodded. "Mr. Weiss, your witness."

The lawyer rose, frowning, thinking on his feet, trying to mount an offense he had received no time to consider. With the sweep of an arm he took in the entire courtroom, from the bench to the back of the room.

"The world has many people in it, Nell. All of these people here could be your friends. These people and many more."

"Alo'so done come," said Lovell. He interlaced his fingers. *"Reckon Nell wanna?"*

Nell was puzzled, but she slowly nodded. *"Reckon."*

"You could share our wonderful world, Nell," said Weiss. "There's so much——"

Lovell translated quickly. *"Nell waw wi' alo'so in erna feliss——"*

"But you have many things to learn."

"Ma'erna lay fo know'n."

Nell nodded, acknowledging the truth of Weiss's words.

"Don't you want that, Nell?"

Nell looked at Weiss, then she let her gaze travel over the many faces in the room, looking from person to person. She seemed to be wrestling with herself, trying to decide if she wanted to be like them or not. As she considered this and the silence lengthened a curious tension began to build in the room. Every person in the court felt Nell's steady searching eyes on them, as if they were under some mute interrogation.

When Nell spoke at last, it was gently, as if she was afraid of giving offense.

"Yo' ha' erna lay——" she said hesitantly.

"You have big things," Lovell translated.

"Yo know'n erna lay——"

"You know big things——"

Nell leaned forward and gripped the edge of the railing. *"Ma' yo' nay seen inna alo'sees——"*

"But you don't look into each other's eyes."

"An yo' aken af'a lilta-lilt." Her voice rose as if filled with passion.

"And you're hungry for quietness."

Nell seemed to relax, relieved that she had said all she knew and had observed about the world beyond the clearing. *"Ah done pass'a missa lye——"*

"I've lived a small life——"

"Ah know'n missa law."

"And I know small things."

Nell looked to the judge and then out at the audience, imploring them with her eyes to believe what she was saying. *"Ma' lilten kine a'fu wi'enja—"*

"But the quiet forest is full of angels—"

"Inna tye'a shie done come Tizrah—"

"In the daytime there comes beauty—"

"Inna tye'a feliss, done come feliss."

"In the nighttime, there comes happiness."

Nell was silent a moment, looking at the people. No one moved, no one made a sound.

"Nay tata fo' Nell," she said quietly.

"Don't be afraid for Nell," said Lovell.

"Nay kee fo' Nell."

"Don't weep for Nell."

"Ah hai' nay erna keena'n yo."

"I have no greater sorrows than you."

She touched her brow with the fingertips of one hand and then brushed her fingers down her cheek, her hand remaining there. Her eyes moved from face to face, offering every person there her love.

Lovell and Olsen both had tears in their eyes. They alone realized what had happened—everything had been turned around. The spectators, those dwellers in the modern world, were helpless. They had the need and Nell had the gift.

The crowd outside the courthouse was larger than the crowd inside, the throng swelled by curiosity seekers, television news crews bristling with equipment, and casual passersby who had been drawn into the excitement. The hearing had ended and the spectators streaming down the courthouse steps added to the congestion on the sidewalk.

When Nell emerged from the red brick building, she had her eyes down, allowing Olsen and Lovell on either side of her to guide her through the crowd, but for a moment, the press of people on the steps trapped her. The TV floodlights opened up and flash bulbs popped. For a moment Nell cowered in fear, pushing back against Lovell's chest.

On the edge of the crowd some kids shouted and pointed. "There she is! There's the wild woman!" Someone started to howl like a wolf and some of the bystanders laughed and jeered.

Nell looked up. Pale, fragile, and profoundly dignified, she met the mocking stares and in an instant the jeers and the laughter faded to an embarrassed, uneasy silence.

Lovell and Olsen led the way, the mass of people parting before them. They looked hard at Nell as she passed, as if her mere presence awed them.

Judge Hazan and Alexander Paley watched from the top of the courthouse steps, following as Nell, Olsen, and Lovell got into Lovell's Jeep.

"Sorry, Professor," said the judge. "I just couldn't do it. I had to let her go where she would be happy."

"You think I wanted her for myself?" said Paley bitterly. His eyes were on the people clustered around the Jeep. He shook his head. "They'll want more. Much more."

EPILOGUE

Five Years Later

The little girl was still asleep, but she was not in her bed. Rather, she was curled in the backseat of the car, her head resting in her father's lap.

"Ruthie still asleep?" Paula Olsen took her eyes off the road long enough to shoot a quick glance over her shoulder.

Lovell looked down at his sleeping daughter, love in his eyes. "Yeah."

"We'll be there any minute."

The road was better now, still unpaved, but the traffic had smoothed it. They rounded the last bend and saw it—the lake, the clearing, the cabin. There were a lot of cars, parked near where the houseboat had once rested.

A bonfire burned in the center of the clearing and within its circle of light Paula could see a crowd of people sitting there, fifty or more. Some had blankets thrown over their shoulders against the chill of the night.

The firelight reached out to the tree line and they could see tents pitched there, some glowing from within with the light of lanterns.

Paula brought the car to a stop and she and her husband got out, Lovell holding the sleeping child in his arms. They looked down into the clearing.

"Gets bigger every year."

Olsen shook her daughter gently. "Wake up, darling. We're at Nell's now."

Ruthie's eyes fluttered and she stirred slightly, then slipped back into a deep sleep.

"She's totally out of it."

"She was awake half last night."

"Come on . . ." Paula led the way down into the clearing, walking toward the crowd and the fire. Some of the people gathered there were talking and laughing softly in the night; some had their eyes closed; others were rocking gently back and forth, humming a tune of sorts. It was a little like a lullaby—there was no beginning, no end, round and round, the sound of calm and quiet.

A familiar face looked up toward them. It was Mary Petersen. She smiled and walked over, all signs of her paralysing depression long gone.

"Hi there," she said. "Welcome back."

"Quite a crowd."

"They keep coming," said Mary. "Does Nell know you're here yet?"

"Not yet."

Mary looked at Ruthie. "My, my, she is getting to be a big girl, isn't she?"

"She was looking forward to seeing Nell so much," said Paula. "Now she won't wake up."

"Where is Nell?" Jerry asked.

Mary pointed. "Right over there."

Nell was sitting cross-legged on the ground in the

middle of the crowd, her pale face warmed by the firelight. She had the old faraway look in her eyes.

Lovell walked toward her, his daughter in his arms. Olsen watched him go, anxious to give him a few moments with Nell before she joined them.

"Jerry is special for Nell," she said. "He means a lot to her."

"So do you, Paula," said Mary.

Olsen watched through the shimmering heat haze as Nell caught sight of Jerry. Her smile ignited and she jumped to her feet to embrace him.

"Oh, sure," said Olsen. "I was the hotshot who was really going to make a difference in her life, remember?"

"But you did," said Mary seriously. "You made an enormous difference in her life. Didn't you know?"

Olsen shook her head. Nell took Ruthie in her arms. The little girl stirred and her eyes opened as Nell smiled down at her. Then she rubbed her face against Ruthie's soft cheek, the child responding with sleepy delight.

"Know what?"

"You were the first."

"The first?"

"You were the first to need her," said Mary.

Nell raised her head, turning to look for Paula, her eyes searching the darkness. Paula gazed and met her look, the two of them looking through the shimmering air. Nell smiled a sweet smile of recognition and nodded, then the smile slipped away.

She looked neither happy nor sad, seeming to accept everything and fear nothing. Those clear eyes reaching out, seeing all the angels in the forest.